I have always liked reading books, even when I tried my hardest to convince my siblings I did not. I stopped pretending at some point and I am truly grateful for that. I was born in Utah and currently reside in a small town that I love. Some of my favorite activities, besides reading and writing, include hiking, fishing, camping, and spending time with my family.

Rise
of the
Lesser Heroes

William Taylor

Rise
of the
Lesser Heroes

Vanguard Press

VANGUARD PAPERBACK

© Copyright 2024
William Taylor

The right of William Taylor to be identified as author of this work
has been asserted by him in accordance with the
Copyright, Designs and Patents Act 1988.

A CIP catalogue record for this title is available from the British
Library.

ISBN 978 1 80016 828 2

This is a work of fiction. Names, characters, businesses, places, events and
incidents are either the products of the author's imagination or used in a
fictitious manner. Any resemblance to actual persons, living or dead, or
actual events is purely coincidental.

Vanguard Press is an imprint of
Pegasus Elliot Mackenzie Publishers Ltd.
www.pegasuspublishers.com

First Published in 2024

Vanguard Press
Sheraton House Castle Park
Cambridge England

Printed & Bound in Great Britain

First, I would like to give a big thanks to all of my family members. Thank you for all your support throughout my life. Secondly, I want to thank my mom and dad for always encouraging me to do the best I can. Lastly, I want to give thanks to my beautiful wife and two children. For they are a well of hope and inspiration that I constantly am grateful for.

For my brother, Steven, who for some reason has some of the weirdest, but best ideas. Without Steven I doubt this book would be more than an idea. He has always been a supporter of my writing, even though he is the one who is the true genius. I feel like much of my job in writing is just to put material on a page. It only takes light after Steven has touched the words. So, thank you for all your hard work and support.

Prologue

Zane whizzed through the air, dodging falling debris from the building. It was at times like this he wished his limits on flight were a little less strict. He changed direction in a flash, narrowly missing a large chunk of cement roughly the size of a car. It fell and crashed onto the asphalt below, leaving a gaping hole in the substrate. The sounds of metal straining to contain the now off-balance building thrummed through the debris filled sky around him. Zane continued to weave through the air, heading towards the top of the leaning building. Luckily it was after hours and there were no civilians in the building. The thought brought him little comfort as he made his way to the top. They failed their mission, and the evidence of this fact was overwhelming as the building began to collapse. Zane willed his body to move faster through the air as he searched the rooftop looking for his friends. He spotted Gliss and Ethan clinging to the building. Gliss screamed as the building shook. Zane dove down towards his comrades, and he landed hard as the building shifted towards him. Zane tumbled to the ground knocking his elbows and knees on the concrete surface.

Shaking his head, Zane pulled himself to his feet and ran to his friends, trying to overcome the daze of landing so hard. It was difficult to run on the slanted, rubble-covered rooftop. Zane's foot slipped on a patch of loose tile, and he hit the ground again, this time he began to slide towards the edge. Zane clawed at the surface and was able to come to a stop. Once again, Zane stood and made his way over to his friends. Gliss grabbed hold of Zane's arm, nearly throwing the two off the building. She cried and hugged him tightly, blood running down the side of her head from a gash. Her suit was torn on the arm sleeves, and she was missing a boot. Ethan called out to them with hands outstretched and Zane noticed that the young man's eyes were completely swollen shut. *Drat!* Zane thought, *He can't use his powers. I'll have to carry them both.* Together Glitter and Zane made their way over to Mirrious who was now clinging to a roof vent. Zane grabbed hold of the man as the building began to crash towards the ground. Glitter screamed and Mirrious clung tightly to Zane as they lost their footing. Accelerating with all his strength, Zane leapt into the air. The added weight of his companions began to drag him down quicker than he'd expected. They plummeted towards the ground at an incredible speed, three screams sounding from the depths of an all-consuming dust cloud.

Chapter 1

Zane

For most of his life Zane was ordinary, which, in itself, was not a bad thing. He tried to do well in school, and he tried to treat everyone with respect. As hard as Zane tried, he often felt like he could be more than he was and dreamed of gaining amazing superpowers. He constantly watched reruns of the great supers fighting the villains of the day. He envisioned what it would have been like to live in the day when real superheroes lived.

It was nearly a hundred years ago when the real superheroes left the planet. Zane wondered what drove them all to leave. The government wasn't against the superheroes. In fact, historical archives are full of ads in the papers looking for new heroes. When the greats fought the evils of the world it was the closest the world had been to achieving world peace.

Well, now society was in shambles. It was just as bad, if not worse, than before the supers. When Zane did develop powers, he wished his power was stronger. Super or not, he was still almost ordinary, not as boring as his parents were, though. Both his parents' powers were closer to hindrances, Zane liked to think of them as anti-powers. His Mom, Mary, for instance, could read enormous books in just minutes, but when she did it left her in a daze, sometimes for days. She could retain the information, but it left her crippled and babbling until she could process the enormous amount of information. Zane's father, Jerry, possessed the power to be places at the wrong time. Most of Zane's life he thought his father's claims of the alleged power was a hoax, something he dreamed up.

Zane did not really believe his father until he was fourteen, when, one afternoon, Zane came home and turned on the T.V. He sifted through the channels and nearly fell out of his chair. On the screen he saw a picture of his father with the label, in all caps "WANTED FOR BANK ROBBERY".

Zane's father burst through the door moments later, claiming that once again he was in the wrong place at the wrong time. The police eventually showed up in force and took his amiable father into custody. It turned out the robbers ran out of the bank the exact moment Jerry walked past. Fearing they would be chased; the robbers handed a bag of money to his father.

Baffled, Jerry looked inside and found it full of money. When his father went to return the money, the guards tried to tase him. Jerry screamed, threw the money at the guards, and ran straight home.

If that wasn't proof enough, it turns out that the cameras had a temporary fault, blacking out for the whole robbery only to turn back on to catch his father throwing the bag of money at the guards. The only photo the cameras outside the bank captured, was one of the robbers giving the bag of money to his father. It took months for the police to catch the real robbers, the damage to Jerry's family already done. Zane's dad became known as an infamous bank robber. Jerry lost his job and was unable to get another one, so his mom took a position at the local college as a professor.

The next year of school was a particularly hard one for Zane. The kids took up calling him "Piggy Bank" and asking him for lunch money. All but one of his friends were told by wary parents to not hang out with Zane. Some of the kids at school even held their hands over pockets and clutched purses as they walked by. There were only a couple of his closest friends that disobeyed their parents' condemnation of his family.

That was over three years ago. Some of the school teasing ebbed a year after the robbery when he developed superpowers of his own. It came as a great relief to his parents that he had not inherited his father's power. Zane woke one day to find his nose pressed against his ceiling, a spider eyeing him from inches away. Zane screamed and, in doing so, sent himself shooting out their second story window. Glass shards cut his face and arms and he remained floating through the neighborhood for hours. The fire department needed to come and pull him down safely.

Today was a special day. Although his father offered to drive him, Zane turned down the offer, assuring his father that he liked to walk. Zane was on his way to take his Flier's License Test. He'd been training hard for over a year now since Zane's powers didn't give him any body protection or extra strength like it did with a very few others. He saved up all the money he could make and, just recently, bought a state-of-the-art flying suit that protected his skin and bones from falls from twenty feet or lower. With his course studies he was also given a radio receiver to communicate with aircraft and other flying personnel. The hardest part had been learning all the rules and procedures of the sky, but, with his mom's help, he eventually passed the written portion of the flier's test.

Zane stepped up to the Flier License Division building; a rather bland, brick exterior with far too bright LED lights (out of date for seventy-five years) nearly covering the entire interior ceiling. The building had far too few windows and the lines in were a chore. However, they were relatively short compared to the lines for the Driver License Division.

Zane opened the door, stepping into the too brightly lit room shielding his eyes from the glaring light. A short stocky woman waved him forward. He took a ticket from her and made his way over to a hard plastic seat in the next room. Zane looked at the piece of paper in his hand, the number two-hundred and seventy-two were printed on the front. Zane wondered when the FLD was going to adopt a technology-friendly interface that could easily be accessed by civilians. It would be much more efficient if the government hired someone to design a new system. Zane didn't even know where someone could buy paper these days, other than toilet paper, and even that was ancient and found mostly in museums or antique stores.

Zane looked around at the people stuck in the small kiosks, sitting with blank expressions typing on hidden keyboards. Screens hung overhead flashing different numbers. As the numbers flashed people stood and walked over. Zane shielded his eyes from the obnoxious lights. The glare shining off the screens was beginning to give him a headache. Zane watched as an old man pulled out a bottle of acetaminophen pills and popped a few in his mouth. He waited for what seemed like an eternity; eventually the screen lit up displaying the number on his paper two seven two. Zane stood searching for the corresponding kiosk; he found it nearly on the other side of the building. Zane walked over to the tall man who stood behind the desk. He looked down at Zane with a disapproving gaze, he handed the man his ticket, the man looked at it and scanned it on his machine. "Mr Whitlock, do you have your papers with you?"

Zane rummaged through his pocket and pulled out his pocketbook; the holographic screen lit up and a moment later Zane found the corresponding papers. He reached up and grabbed the papers from the machine, the tall man held out his hand and took the glowing blue folder. He held it over his computer for a moment before the program was accepted and the papers formed on the screen of the man's computer. "So, what can I do for you Mr Whitlock?"

"I need to take my flier's test today." The man looked him up and down, then sighed, "Okay, wait here for a moment." The man turned and went into an unseen room, he returned a moment later holding out a bright orange suit and helmet towards Zane, who took the suit from the man

"Go down the hallway, there is a changing room on the right, the flight-testing center is across the hallway, go through the sliding door and your flight instructor will meet you there." He pointed to a hallway that was practically glowing, Zane walked towards the hallway that looked as if it consumed the sun. Squinting, he found his way down the hallway and into the men's changing room. Zane quickly changed into the ridiculous suit and placed his clothes and belongings in a small locker that scanned his palm print into memory. He made his way back out into the glaring light, but this time the helmet's auto tint function kicked in and the light became manageable. Zane headed through the sliding door. The room inside was massive; it contained a full city block with pedestrians, cars, signs, and other flying aircraft circling above.

"Mr Whitlock." Zane turned to find a man dressed in the same ridiculous orange suit.

"Uh yes sir," he said. The man gave him a thumbs up, "Okay, are you ready?" he asked in a relaxed tone. "I guess," Zane said hesitating.

"All right man, let's get going. By the way my name's Zack." Zack rose into the air his body seemed to be vibrating violently.

"Are you all right?" Zane asked

"Sure dude, this is how I fly. I don't feel it any more I kind of just feel numb. What about you? Why aren't you flying?"

Zane looked at him and, without explanation, he took off running. Zane couldn't figure out how to fly from a standing position. He tried for weeks after his powers came but he couldn't replicate the action he performed in his sleep. It wasn't until he had been running and tripped that he was able to fly again. Zane ran, got up to full speed, and tripped himself. His body began to fly at the same speed he had been running at.

"I get it, you need a running start. Cool. Everyone has their way. Turn your radio on and follow me."

Zane reached up to the helmet and twisted a small knob. Static fuzzed in his ear a moment then Zack's voice came in loud and kind of clear; it sounded like he was talking while driving on a really bumpy road.

"All right bro, let's test your zero to sixty time."

Zane never tested his zero to sixty time, there simply wasn't space where he lived, plus there was a no-flying ordinance in the part of the city he lived in.

19

You couldn't fly without an adult, unless you had your license.

Zane followed Zack through the air, to a large football field. Zack landed on the far side and Zane decided to hover a couple of inches off the ground next to him.

"All right, you have until the end of the football field to reach sixty miles an hour; that is the minimum requirement to enter any major flyways in the city."

"All right, let's do it," Zane heard himself saying.

Zane saw a speedometer appear in his helmet's interface. He took off faster than he'd ever tried to go before. Ten, twenty, twenty-five, thirty. Each number flashed in his helmet. Zane passed the middle of the football field, thirty-five. Zane pushed his body forward and sweat began to form on his forehead. Forty, forty-three, forty-six, forty-nine point eight.

Zane ran out of field and pulled up, trying to avoid the folded bleacher chairs. He heard Zack let out a whistle through the speakers.

"Want to try again?" Zack asked him.

"Yes."

Four tries later, Zane stood hands on his knees breathing hard.

"Well, you broke fifty on that last run. Um... I'm going to go ahead and say you passed. Fifty is close enough. Just stick with the lower altitudes and you should be fine until you gain enough speed to join the rest of the traffic."

Zane nodded and Zack took off vibrating in a different direction. "Let's test the rest of your skills"

Zane followed and passed the communications portions with ease. Zack pointed up and Zane followed the other man up to the top of the dome. Raising his visor, Zack spoke to Zane. "Now we're going to test your pull-up response time. What you're going to do is take a nosedive and you're going to pull up when I tell you. If you can pass this last portion, you will be flying home today." Zack gave a thumbs up and began to plummet.

Zane followed behind him. The speedometer in his helmet reached two hundred and thirteen miles an hour. A gust blew by him and threatened to send him in a chaotic spin, but Zane held the position. Zack began to level out and Zane followed him. Zane began to slow down as he pulled out of the dive. Out of nowhere, Zack began to dive.

Zane decided the risk was worth it and followed Zack into another dive.

"I wasn't expecting you to follow me, bro. Good job on your response time. You can pull up whenever you're comfortable. I just like to feel the adrenaline in my veins."

The comment distracted him, and Zane yelled in his helmet as the ground rushed towards him. He absently heard Zack let out a shout of joy. Straining, Zane pulled out of the dive, his feet scraped the dirt field below him before he gained a couple feet of altitude. Breathing hard and doused in a cold sweat, Zane landed back in front of the sliding doors next to Zack. Zack pulled off his helmet, "Bro, that was lit!" he said, holding out a fist.

Zane completed the fist-bump, and Zack dismissed him holding out a blue folder. Zane took the folder and headed back inside with a smile and a nod. He pulled off the gear and placed it in the bin marked 'used suits'. He finished pulling on his shoes, then headed back to the tall man behind the kiosk. Zane handed the man the blue folder, he accepted it and reviewed the results. "Congratulations, Mr Whitlock, you are cleared to fly." Zane smiled and the man began typing on his computer. A moment later he held out a holographic card, Zane took the card from him and looked at it. His photo was terrible; he looked like a villain.

"Hey, is there any way I can change the photo?" he asked the man.

"No, this is the photo that you will have until you turn twenty-five. Please exit to the right," he gestured to a door that had a sign that read 'exit' in bright green. Zane took the license and placed it into his wallet. Instead of exiting to the right door, Zane went and changed into his flying suit first.

He stepped into the daylight and breathed in. Smiling, Zane tripped down the stairs and began flying. As he rose up into the air, the facility became a speck. Zane set his destination to Gliss's house; she would want to see his license. Zane made his way through the city, watching the cars sitting in traffic. Zane made sure to check his radar and radio as he flew, he found the view of the city from above beautiful. Zane felt like he could see the whole world. He flew with the air currents that tugged on him gently. The GPS beeped, signaling he was at his destination. Zane descended from his perch above the world and spiraled down in a controlled loop. He landed on the front steps of his best friend's house.

Zane had known Gliss his entire life; the two of them did everything together. Zane removed his helmet and tried his best to smooth out his hair. The unruly strands refused to be manipulated by anything including his hands. Zane wondered if it would be better to leave his helmet on to avoid the humiliation of Gliss's laughter. Zane finally moved to the door and gave a none too subtle knock. Moments later, the familiar face of Gliss bobbed into view. She kept her red hair in a tight bun that sat off to one side of her head. Gliss was not very tall but, what she lacked in height she made up for in beauty. Zane wondered if it was weird to think she was beautiful because, after all, she was his best friend, but he couldn't lie to himself. Her green, vibrant eyes seemed to gaze into his very soul. Gliss always wore old forgotten band tee shirts and jeans.

"So, did you pass?" Gliss asked excitedly. Zane pulled out his new license from a pocket in his suit.

"Yep," he said beaming, holding the license out towards her face. She snatched the license from his hand and began to examine it. She gasped as her eyes fell on the photo that appeared in the top right corner.

"Wow! you look hideous, how did they get you to look so bad?" she said in awe. Zane's cheeks began to burn red with embarrassment. Gliss handed back the license and Zane quickly put the license back in his pocket.

Gliss ruffled her hand through his hair. "I understand how they got the picture to look so bad, they took it after they made you fly through a tornado right?"

Zane snickered, "Yeah I know, the picture is bad but at least I got my license."

"You're right, I should be congratulating you instead, so, good job. So, when are you going to take me flying?" Gliss asked, batting her eyes at him. Zane hadn't thought about it; she was right, he could fly one other person. Legally.

Zane didn't respond quick enough as Gliss delivered a nudge to his ribs. "Yeah, sorry, do you have a suit? Protocol says you need to have a no-fliers suit in order for me to fly you safely." Zane said, pulling on two clips that hung from his shoulders. Smiling, Gliss closed her front door.

Zane waited on the front steps and listened to Gliss shout at her mom she was going flying with Zane. Gliss stood in the pinkest suit Zane had ever seen.

"So do you like it?" she said twirling around,

"It's definitely bright," Zane said, holding back the urge to shield his eyes from the bright color.

"Thanks. I knew you would like it," she said with a twinkle in her eye.

"Let's go, come on, I can't wait any longer," Gliss said, pulling on her matching pink helmet. Zane helped Gliss set up her communications settings on her helmet and, a moment later, Zane took the corresponding loops on Gliss's suit and connected them with his, Zane felt his heart pounding. This was the closest he had ever stood to Gliss for any length of time.

"So, how do we take off?" Gliss asked, her voice playing through Zane's built-in speakers. Instead of replying, Zane fell forwards off the front steps, not used to the added weight. Zane found Gliss only inches above the cement. She let out a shriek and Zane apologized to her, before beginning to ascend. The two of them took off towards the sky. Zane's helmet registered their speed as they climbed. The display numbers read a lame fourteen miles per hour. He groaned audibly and Gliss asked him what was wrong. Zane lied and told her that he was sore from his test earlier. He regretted it as Gliss told him they could fly another day.

"Na, it's fine, we could head back to my house to show my mom and dad my license. You could stay for dinner if you'd like," Zane said through his helmet.

"Sure, I'm sure my parents wouldn't mind, I will ask just to be sure. I'm going to shut off our coms now." Zane held his hand out in front of her helmet with a gloved thumbs up. Zane began to gain altitude; his speedometer remained at fourteen miles an hour. He said a series of commands to his helmet and, a moment later, his house was plugged into the GPS. The voice

25

guidance played through his speakers. The yellow holographic arrow came into view, Zane reached out passing his hand through the illusion, the light dispersed around his glove continuing to point the direction to his home.

Zane turned, following the arrow. He flew for some time wondering how long it took to ask for your parents' permission. It wasn't until he saw the flashing blue light in the corner of his display that he realized that it was Gliss signaling to him she was finished. Zane turned the communications knob on the side of his helmet. A moment later the blue light faded and Gliss's voice came online.

"Finally! I've been trying to tell you that it's absolutely beautiful from up here. Can you go any faster?"

Zane smiled; he knew that going down he could speed excessively so, in response, Zane began to dive down following the arrow that was pointing slightly down. The two of them fell, gaining speed as they rushed towards the ground.

Gliss giggled and squealed as they fell. Zane pulled up and their speed began to plain out.,

"I wish I could fly," Gliss said longingly.

"It's pretty cool, right?"

The GPS beeped, again signaling their arrival. Zane landed in his front yard. He unhooked the support straps and Gliss stepped away from him. She turned and pulled off her helmet. Her red hair stuck out at odd angles; it was a complete mess, but Zane was happy to see her smile.

She grinned from ear to ear.

"I guess I won't have to take the bus anymore," she said excitedly. Zane nearly fell over. The thought of him arriving at school with hundreds of eyes watching, as Gliss in her hot pink flight suit landing strapped to his front was overwhelmingly embarrassing.

"Yay! I can't wait" Zane said unenthusiastically. She gave him a soft punch in the shoulder.

"What? You don't want to take me to school?" Gliss asked him, her eyes gleaming up at him.

"No, it's nothing, I will take you, no problem," he said, waving his hands in front of him as if to dispel his real feelings.

"Great! I'm so excited! Now, let's go show your mom and dad your license." Zane got excited remembering that he actually got it.

"Yeah, let's do it".

Together they walked up the front steps, Zane pulled open the front door holding it for Gliss, she stepped inside with a spring in her step. Zane followed and found his mom and dad both lounging on the couch with their eyes closed.

"Hi, Mr and Mrs Whitlock!" Gliss said beaming.

Zane's parents shot up from their positions on the leather couch. "Oh, hello, Glisandra, you look radiant today," Zane's Mom said with a smile.

"Thank you!"

Jerry looked at Gliss and, with eyebrows raised, said, "I like the new look, its…" His father froze looking for the right word which Marry filled in for him.

"Vibrant," she said quickly. Jerry nodded, and Gliss beamed.

Zane's parents were the only people he knew that could get away with calling Gliss by her full name. She even forbade teachers at school to use her full name. Zane himself never tried calling her Glisandra and he probably wouldn't risk the potential consequences. For now, and for the foreseeable future, Zane would just stick to Gliss.

"So, are we lucky enough to have you for dinner tonight?" Zane's mother asked.

"You sure are"

"Great, would you mind joining me in the kitchen? I could use your expertise on the dish I'm preparing." Gliss agreed, leaving Zane and his father sitting across from each other. They sat for some time before his dad asked how his test had gone. Zane proudly whipped out the license and held it out for his father to inspect. The usual conversation ensued about the photograph they had chosen. After seeing the image, his father had wandered into the kitchen to show his mother the horrific image. This nearly destroyed Zane's license, as the three of them had begun laughing in the kitchen and his father had lost grip on the I.D. and it had fallen dangerously close to the stove's flames.

Zane took the license back and placed it securely in his wallet. The evening moved on with lots of laughter and jokes, before coming to an end.

Zane stepped out onto his balcony followed by Gliss. She zipped up her suit and walked forward to stand beside him. They stood for a moment watching the last few rays of the sunset turn the clouds into purple and orange pastels against the city skyline.

"Thanks for having me over tonight. I always enjoy your family's company."

"It's nothing. I'm sure they like you more than me sometimes. So, is it time to get you home?"

Gliss smiled before sliding her helmet on. She stepped in close to him. Zane's heart began to pound before realizing she was letting him strap her in for the flight. After he was sure she was secure, Zane dove off the balcony and, in a swooping arch narrowly missing the house across from them, Zane rose into the sky. He listened to Gliss breathe softly through the helmet's communications system. They glided through the sky looking at the glittering lights below them, Gliss spoke.

"Zane?"

"Yeah, Gliss?"

"I just wanted to say thanks for the incredible night. I really enjoyed myself."

"Yeah, anytime, Gliss."

"I don't want to fly with anyone else, you know that, right?"

"I remember, Gliss. You don't trust anybody except me."

"You better not forget that," she said forcefully.

"I won't," Zane said defensively.

He landed on Gliss's front step. He unhooked her and removed his helmet so he could get some fresh air. His front screen began to fog up in the cool evening air. Gliss pulled her helmet off and held it off to one side resting it on her hip. Gliss stepped in close, she looked up at him, her emerald, green eyes reflecting the moonlight. Zane swallowed hard. She rested her head on his chest. Zane had no idea what to do so he did what felt right, he stood with arms straight and back stiff. He must have done something right as Gliss nuzzled in closer, Zane tried to flex his chest muscles, but nothing happened. Gliss pulled away and stepped up onto her tippy toes then planted a kiss right on his lips.

Zane just about died, as his body shot backwards, zooming in reverse at a crazy speed. His visor display showed a maximum acceleration of three Gs and a top speed of seventy-five miles per hour; but his mind was racing far beyond this. Zane yelped and tried to regain his composure, slowly coming to a stop. When he looked back to the front porch, Gliss had disappeared and had been replaced by a large pile of red glitter. Zane awkwardly flew back to her front porch. During his unexpected take off, he'd dropped his helmet. Zane began to rummage through the large pile of glitter, sending up clouds that swirled around in the air. Before he knew it a hand shot out holding his helmet towards him.

"Gliss, is that you?" Zane asked, accepting the helmet from the hand.

"Yes," a muffled voice said from the depths of the glitter pile. Zane reached into the pile and pulled Gliss from within the shimmering heap. She wouldn't look him in the eye, embarrassed. So, Zane did the only thing that made sense, he dipped her and planted a kiss of his own. A quiet crunch came from behind Gliss, and pink glitter exploded everywhere, swelling around them like a princess-themed pyroclastic flow. In a split second it threatened to consume them both. Zane lifted Gliss and hovered above the ground, glitter streaming off them as they rose slowly toward the moon.

"Gliss, can I ask you something?" Zane said, holding her close.

"You're wondering about the glitter, huh?"

"Yeah... Are you... um..."

"It's kind of a long story. Can I tell you tomorrow on our way to school?"

"Sure, um... thanks I, uh... I didn't know how to, um, show you what you meant to me like you showed me."

"Well, don't get too used to it, you're going to have to earn the next one." Gliss said, thankful for the darkness hiding her burning red cheeks.

"How long did it take for me to earn the first one?" Zane asked curiously.

Gliss considered this then responded, "five years."

"Five years! I don't know if I can wait that long."

"Well, you're just going to have to wait and see," she said, her cheeks returning to normal. Zane agreed, he waved goodbye as she walked through the front door.

Zane could hear Gliss's mother yelling something about no more glitter as he flew. Zane smiled as he soared away. Tomorrow couldn't come fast enough.

Chapter 2

Glissandra

Gliss stood in front of the large turbo-charged fan her father built into the basement. Both Gliss and her parents were quite confused when her power manifested. The turbo fan was her father's way of attempting to support her. Her father, Dale Dunlap, was one of the majority of people born without powers but made up for that fact by becoming super handy at just about everything. Gliss's mother, Denise Dunlap, on the other hand, had a sixth sense. She could see and monitor cleanliness. This led to exhibiting some OCD tendencies and calling home whenever she could feel they forgot to make their beds in the morning. This created tension between Gliss and her mother. Dale tried to smooth things over with the gift of the turbo charged fan that wooshed all of the glitter and dust in the whole basement level (which included Gliss's room) out of the house. It was sweet of him, and it helped her not spend hours cleaning up glitter before bed. And it also helped that she didn't feel itchy all over, like she just got home from the prom. The fan helped in a lot of ways, but Gliss couldn't help wonder where the glitter would end up and who else would have to deal with it. The image of ats at the dump waiting for some tasty tidbits to come out of a garbage shoot and, instead, getting flooded with glitter, briefly filled her thoughts.

When Gliss's powers first manifested, everyone had been oblivious, annoyed, and quite curious about the many glitter explosions someone seemed to have been pranking them with. Her younger brother, Travis, was the prime suspect. They always seemed to happen when something exciting or distracting was happening which made it really hard to investigate. But, each time, Gliss remembered stepping on something crunchy and hearing a crack like an eggshell underfoot. This was followed by a huge glitter explosion of various sizes and colors. They finally discovered that it was Gliss's emotions creating the small glass orb glitter bombs and that she could choose not to step on them inside the house producing much less chaos.

Gliss wandered into her room pulling out her cellphone. She had too much to think about after tonight and she couldn't stop the color from rising to her cheeks over and over again. How long would she make Zane wait before kissing him again. It could be fun to tease him, but Gliss knew she wouldn't be able to put it off for long after all, as she too was really excited about the night's development. She thought about how she would greet him the next morning as she flopped on her bed. She could pretend like nothing was different or she could jump right in and hold his hand. She knew if she was going to make a gutsy move like that, she would have to have much better composure than she had right now. Zane would definitely make fun of her if her face reached even a light shade of pink. She would happily settle for pink now because she could tell her cheeks were in full tomato red. At least her brother was off at a sleepover, so he hadn't seen the night's events or attempt to tease her.

She realized she was scrolling back and forth between her apps and had been doing so for some time. She finally picked her "Tuned" app and began listening to her "calm down" playlist.

This gave her less to do with her fingers, as she had nothing to scroll through, but she hoped listening to something would distract her from remembering what happened over and over again. But man! Zane had been smooth! He caught her off guard with that dip kiss and, despite his clammy hands, it was magical. So much so that it almost made her forget that his heart had been dancing a jig when she snuggled in. Oh, and how rigid his body went! It felt like she was hugging a statue. She giggled. Then she thought about how embarrassed she should be for making such bold moves. What was she thinking? She sure hoped it came across as confident and not cheesy.

Her palm found its way to her face where it rested. Glancing at the clock she could see one a.m. glowing in the corner of her phone's screen. One thing was for sure, she probably wouldn't be getting any sleep tonight.

There was a soft but defined knock at Gliss's door. Gliss pulled her headphones out of one ear in time to hear, "Honey. Honey, are you awake?" Gliss's mother's voice called out.

Gliss was pretty sure her mother could sense that her sheets were in disarray and moving every time she rolled to the other side of the bed.

"Sorry, Mom, I'll stop messing with the sheets. You can go back to bed now," she responded.

"Honey, do you need to talk about something? Does it maybe have something to do with Zane dropping you off?"

"You can't tell her we were watching," Gliss heard her father say under his breath, followed by a very loud thud. Gliss rolled her eyes. So, their moment was not as private as she thought. At this point in time, Gliss wished her parents weren't so involved in her life.

"I heard that," she called back.

After another loud thump, her mother's voice, angry, whispered,

"Go back upstairs, I am handling this. Go do something in the kitchen."

"You know I think I could handle it too, though," her father defended, as his voice faded up the stairwell.

"Honey, can I come in? Are you okay? " her mother's voice called again.

"Doing great, Mom. Can I go to bed now? It's pretty late."

There was a moment of silence before her mother called again,

"You know I think your rug is wrinkled on the one side again. I think I better just come in and straighten it before you go to bed."

"Mom, I thought you were trying to get better. If you fix it, you won't be making any progress. Besides I know you are just trying to make an excuse to talk some more."

There was a brief silence before her dad's voice reappeared "Glissandra, I made French toast!"

Gliss facepalmed for what seemed to be the thousandth time that night and suddenly realized that she was starving. The door slowly opened and Gliss could see two very excited parents smiling from ear to ear. Her father was wearing a "kiss the cook" apron over his jammies and gripping a spatula in one hand. *Oh boy,* Gliss thought, *what have I done.* Gliss found herself being hauled up the stairs by her parents. She couldn't protest. She opened the door, inferring to her parents she was also open to talking. In reality, that was the last thing she wanted to do at the moment. Maybe French toast would open her up to the idea.

Gliss took her place at the table and moments later she was staring at a steaming pile of French toast with ten different syrup flavors soon joining the stack. Her mother slid a plate in front of her along with a fork and knife. Both parents joined Gliss with plates of their own, together they dug into the stack. Soon all that remained were three plates slathered in different syrups, crumbs and pools of butter. Sitting back, Gliss found herself feeling happy. What was the big deal? She could tell her parents anything. It just took French toast to do it.

"So, tell us when this development happened? How long have you two been dating?" her mother said, leaning her chin in her hands. The faint sound of glass hitting the floor came from under her chair. Immediately, Gliss's Dad stood up and fetched a bin. He placed it under her feet and the glass spheres began to fall into the container.

"I guess it just sorta happened tonight," Gliss said

"Oh really? I would have thought the two of you would have kissed years ago," Her Dad said, intrigued. "Really Dad, tonight was the first time," Gliss responded.

"We're just so happy for you both. I could see the way you looked at him," her mom responded. "Mom!"

"What? I'm just saying. He is pretty cute." Gliss wanted to hide back in her room. What had she been thinking? Gliss tried to conceal her face in her hands.

"What is it? Did we say something wrong?"

Her Dad asked, placing a hand on her shoulder. "No, I'll be fine. I'm just trying to sort out all my thoughts and feelings. Thanks for the French toast Daddy."

"Anytime, butterfly," he said leaning in and placing a kiss on her cheek.

"Denise, honey, let's let Glissandra get to bed."

"Okay fine, Dale," her mother said, emphasizing his name. Begrudgingly, Denise let her husband drag her upstairs. Gliss placed her plate in the dishwasher and activated the cleaning sequence. Instead of buying a sound machine, the Dunlaps bought a dishwasher. It helped her mother fall asleep at night knowing that cleaning was happening which seemed to help ease her mother's OCD.

Gliss flipped off the lights and walked back downstairs to the basement. She groaned as she realized she left her glitter spheres in the container at the table. Gliss made her way back upstairs and picked up the container. It was nearly full. This must have been the most she had ever made in one sitting. Gliss went back downstairs and pulled out the sorting machine her father designed specifically to organize her spheres by size, weight, and color. She dumped the bin into the machine and a low swooshing sound came from the machine as it began to organize the spheres and deposit them around in different containers around her room. She watched as they rolled around the different tubes. Gliss flopped back onto her bed. It was nearly three o'clock. She groaned and smothered her head under her pillow. Gliss began to feel drowsy and decided that it would be good to get some rest. She let sleep come and began to snore.

Chapter 3

General Studies

Zane woke up to the same alarm he had been waking up to his whole life; his mother clattering pots and pans, as she pulled out the specific one she was searching for. Zane rolled out of bed, his brown hair a rumpled mess. Zane instinctively walked down the hall and into the bathroom. He brushed his teeth, combed his hair, and made sure to put deodorant on, before he left his hand hovered over his father's cologne. *What's the worst that could happen?* he thought to himself. Zane spritzed a small amount on his singular chest hair. The smell was very masculine but, overall, pleasing.

Zane ran back to his room and dressed himself for the day. He chose a shirt that he'd only worn once that week. He sniffed it and checked for excessive wrinkles. He hesitated then decided it would get wrinkled by his tight-fitting flight suit anyway. Zane pulled the shirt on and began to put on the flight suit. He finished and headed downstairs, helmet in hand. His mother waved at him, and Zane stepped over, embracing her quickly. She gave him a kiss on the cheek.

"Well, don't you smell nice this morning? Did something happen last night?"

Zane froze and he recognized his mistake; the cologne was a dead give away.

"Maybe something involving Glissandra?"

"I um…" Zane's cheeks began to burn. He completely forgot how to talk for a moment.

Zane's dad walked into the room and asked, "so what are we talking about on this glorious morning?"

"Good morning, honey. We were just talking about Zane dating Glissandra!"

Zane's jaw dropped; he couldn't believe the accusations that were being tossed around like a crumpled old newspaper.

"Mom! Dad! I can't believe you!"

"Well, it must be true from your reaction, right? Also, Denise called me last night to inform me of the night's events. She even sent me the footage recorded from the video doorbell. You were great. But what was with all the glitter?"

"Okay, well, I'm glad we all enjoyed last night, some of us more than others, but I really have to get going," Zane said walking towards the door.

His father caught his arm as he strode past, "sorry, son, we didn't mean to snoop. We just like to be involved in your life."

Zane stood for a moment then embraced his dad; his mother joined in on the group hug. The embrace ended and Zane was allowed passage. He waved goodbye to his parents and fell off the front steps. A moment later he began to rise up towards the sky. Zane spoke a command to his helmet and his morning playlist began playing. He tried to forget about the embarrassing morning start.

Zane felt better as he approached Gliss's house. He landed and turned off his music. Zane noticed for the first time the video doorbell. Zane cursed the machine as he knocked on the door. Denise pulled the door open and ushered Zane inside. She pulled out a chair and, with a smile, gestured for him to sit down. Zane complied and sat down on the plastic chair. His suit squeaked with every move so Zane tried to hold as still as he could. "Sorry, Zane, Glissandra is running a little behind this morning."

"It's fine. How are you doing, Denise?"

"I'm just peachy. You smell good today."

"Thanks," Zane said. He was beginning to feel awkward just sitting alone in the Dunlap's kitchen.

"How is your mom doing?" Denise asked.

Zane wanted to give a witty retort, knowing the two of them had been conspiring all night, but he held his tongue.

"She is doing well, keeping busy."

"That's nice." Zane felt relief flood through him as he saw Gliss climbing the stairs from the basement.

"Good morning, Mom. Good morning, Zane," she said with a wave.

"Good morning, Gliss. Are you ready for school?"

Gliss eyed her mother with a wary look. "Mm hm. Sure am! I'm ready when you are."

"Don't you want to eat breakfast first?" Gliss's mother asked.

"Sorry, Mom, I don't think Zane and I have that kind of time today, maybe another day, all right?"

"All right, you two get going."

Denise leaned in and whispered in Zane's ear, "take care of my little girl for me, okay?" Zane looked at her and nodded, implying he would take care of Gliss.

Together Gliss and Zane made their way to the door, and they waved a goodbye towards Denise. The door closed behind them. Zane grabbed Gliss's hand and pulled her down the steps and around the corner, making sure the two of them were not visible to the recording doorbell. When he was sure they were not being watched, he let go of her hand, but her hand did not let go of his, her fingers still gripped his now open palm. Zane closed his fingers back around hers and looked at her, hoping she wasn't furious with him.

"Hi Zane, it's good to see you again so soon." She gave a brief smile. It wasn't until then that Zane noticed her eyes were bloodshot and her hair wasn't as pulled together as it usually was.

"It's good to see you too, Gliss. Are you feeling all right?" She yawned and tried to cover her mouth nonchalantly.

"Yeah. It was a long night at my house."

"Did it have anything to do with all the glitter?"

She hesitated, "yes and no… It had more to do with this." Gliss said, raising their intertwined hands.

"Oh… Yeah, my morning was pretty weird."

"Moms, am I right?" Gliss said, rolling her eyes. Zane nodded and agreed with the statement.

"So… what is this?" Zane asked, raising their hands once more into the air.

"What kind of question is that? We're boyfriend, girlfriend, dummy."

Zane smiled at the remark, even sleep-deprived Gliss was fiery; it was something that Zane liked about her.

"Hey, we are going to be late, let's get flying," Gliss said, letting her hand fall from his.

She turned around waiting for Zane to hook up the straps. Zane stepped forward and quickly clipped the supports on, a moment later he fell backwards. Zane felt his back hit the ground softly, he had learned from his mistake yesterday. Zane began to soar upwards. He twisted the communication knob on his helmet.

"So, what is this long story about glitter?" he asked.

He was surprised to hear snoring coming through the speakers. He laughed to himself and switched the knob off.

Travel to school was significantly shorter than a car ride because Zane was allowed to take a more direct route and avoid traffic. He watched the cars below him following their restricted grid guidelines. He grinned and spread his arms wide, loving the freedom he felt.

The school came into view. Its nine separate buildings connected with a central courtyard laid out below him in a pattern he had never realized they formed from the ground.

Each of the buildings specialized in a different field like buildings at higher universities specialized in different subjects. Years ago, the school district united and held meetings to change the way schooling was approached. The council decided instead of going to elementary, middle, and high schools, they would incorporate all the material one would learn in the twelve years by the end of middle school in only seven years; the remaining five years would be spent specializing in one field or another.

Zane was grateful for the change but, unfortunately for Zane, his seventh-grade year was the same year his father had been known as a bank robber. To put some distance between himself and the other kids, Zane had enrolled in the "General Study" program. He was now in his senior year; his graduating class made up of only thirty students, Gliss being one of them. Zane felt guilty when he thought about it. He knew that Gliss had chosen the same program because she was such a good friend to him and didn't want to leave him all alone. Zane knew that she had so much potential and would have easily done very well in most of the other programs. She frequently read the material from some of the other programs and practiced taking the exams "just to keep her wits sharp" as she put it.

The other programs consisted of Business, Engineering/Architecture, Medical, Law, Military, Art, History, and Academics; each housed in a separate building. Inside each building there were options to study and experience the hundreds of careers in various specializations that fit under the umbrella of the building's field. In General Studies, Zane had decided to pick the career of three-dimensional printing technician. He actually enjoyed the program. Gliss had enrolled in Clothing Manufacturing/ Tech. Their school year was nearly up, and Zane was feeling a bit down. He truly wished he had another year under his belt. However, there were some things that couldn't be altered, one of them being time.

Zane began his descent and nudged Gliss with one finger prodding her in the neck, her body stiffening as she began to wake up. Zane probably could have waited to wake her until they had landed. He tried to imagine what it would feel like to wake up while flying at such a height. He reached up and twisted the communications knob. Gliss's voice came in a moment later.

"Sorry Zane," she said through a yawn.

"You're fine. You looked tired this morning. I hope I didn't scare you too much by waking you up."

"Don't be silly. This is the best I have slept in ages," she said while stretching her hands and arms out from her body. Her hand disrupted Zane's vision just long enough for him to miscalculate their distance from the ground. Zane's foot caught on a particularly high cut of grass sticking out from a knoll. The friction with his boot was enough to send them falling forward. They hit the ground and began to roll down the hill. The two of them came to a standstill.

Zane's backpack laid a good fifteen feet from them and he could hear laughter coming through Gliss's helmet.

"That was wonderful! Can we do it again?" she said through tears that sprouted from the corners of her eyes. She cried every time she laughed too hard.

Zane tried to ignore the feeling of eyes watching him, but it was inevitable there was no escaping the prying eyes of others. He learned that the hard way earlier this morning. Privacy was nothing more than a myth.

Zane awkwardly stood and unlatched the connection cables attached to Gliss. She stepped away and together they walked over and retrieved his lost backpack. Gliss pulled off her helmet and Zane followed soon after. Gliss reached out and took Zane's free hand in hers, holding it tight. Her touch had a soothing effect and he felt more relaxed. Zane had imagined the touch would be more exhilarating. Not wanting this sensation to change, he stood a little closer to her as they walked.

Gliss reached out and opened the door to the General Studies building. A rush of warm air washed over them and awkwardly they tried to step through the door at the same time. Zane ended up walking behind Gliss's outstretched hand, his hand still clutching hold of hers. He pulled up beside her and tried to figure out a

47

better way of fitting through the next door that stood in their path.

No new ideas came to him and the two of them ended up doing the same awkward dance through the next door. Glad to not have another door to go through Zane let out a sigh of relief.

"Well, we made it!" Gliss said triumphantly. She guided him down a well-lit hallway and to a glowing pink locker. Gliss temporarily let go of Zane's hand and placed her palm down on the scanner. A blue light flashed then the automated lock clicked, and the door hissed open. Gliss unzipped her flight suit, revealing a black shirt portraying a hand clutching a beating heart.

Zane didn't really appreciate the image. The words above the image read, FRAGILE in all caps, each word oozed down suggesting they were made of blood.
Gliss seeing the face Zane was making at her shirt asked, "What? Don't you like it?"

Zane, not wanting their new level of friendship to be built on lies, told her the blunt and honest truth, "I actually dislike it very much. It's creepy."

Gliss just shrugged her shoulders and put her suit inside her locker.

"I thought you would have better tastes" She finally said.

Zane didn't think taste had anything to do with not liking the article of clothing. Gliss reached down and took his hand again. The hallways were relatively empty. The building only had a hundred or so students and covered twenty or so acres. Zane and Gliss walked for some time before reaching his locker which was located a couple city blocks in distance away from hers. Finally, they reached his locker and Zane opened it, then he removed his suit, placing it inside along with his helmet.

A wave of cologne hit Zane's nose. Trapped in the suit the fragrance was only now able to disperse and it did so strongly. Gliss took a step back from him as she was buffeted by the scent of cologne. Eventually the smell became bearable and Gliss stepped in close once more.

"So, did you drink the bottle of cologne? Or did you simply bathe in it?" she asked him incredulously. Zane's cheeks began to fill with color as he had indeed made the wrong decision to put on the unfamiliar product. He smiled sheepishly before answering.

"Sorry, I thought it might be nice."

"Well, I don't really enjoy the smell but since I like the person wearing it, I will bear it today."

"Only if you promise to wear that shirt as little as possible after today," Zane said pointing at her shirt.

She gave him a sour look then agreed to the compromise. Zane felt like she was the only one who gave up something they actually liked. Zane really didn't like the cologne. He sighed then told her she could wear the shirt, but she just shook her head and said she wanted to keep her end of the deal. Which only made Zane feel worse; he would have to make it up to her later.

The two of them made their way to their first class. They had designed their schedule so that they could spend all day together. It had left them both in an odd position, each taking half of their classes in each other's specified field but, overall, it had been a pretty good year.

"So, we have some free time before first period. Why don't you tell me about the glitter?" Zane said. Gliss froze in place. Zane stopped to look at her, but she cast her eyes down looking at her feet.

"Not a good time?" Zane asked she nodded her head.

"Can I tell you after school?" she asked him, looking embarrassed.

"Sure, but you have to promise to tell me this time. No getting out of it by snoring."

"I do not snore!" she said indignantly, "but I *will* tell you this time. You have my promise. Cross my heart and hope to die." She said the last part with a mischievous smile while crossing the bleeding heart on the t-shirt. Zane grimaced and decided not to push the snoring issue.

A gentle chime rang through the empty corridors, signaling it was time for classes to begin. A short while later, students began to emerge from their hiding places, and the hallways began to look a little more like a functioning high school. Gliss pulled Zane's hand and he reluctantly followed her.

Their first class of the day was perhaps the most boring for Zane; Beginning of Clothing Design. If it weren't for Gliss, Zane knew he would have failed the class miserably. She practically did his homework for him. She constantly had to remind him that she really didn't mind doing the homework for the both of them. That was as long as Zane kept his end of the bargain when it reached classes about three-dimensional printing, which he had done so far. The problem about their arrangement that neither of them had wanted to acknowledge, was end of year finals. They couldn't take the final exams for each other, and the end of the school year was quickly approaching. Zane would have to bring up the problem today, even if Gliss gave him puppy eyes and begged him to put it off for another couple weeks. Zane and Gliss walked in through the large metal door. A green light flashed as they entered declaring them free of weapons and other objects, including, but not limited to personal cell phones, any audio devices, drugs, and/or toxic materials. Zane had never understood the reason for the last one. He couldn't imagine a situation where someone would willingly want to be close to toxic materials, let alone actually desire to carry them around.

Gliss tugged him along and together they took their seats. There were only a total of five students in the whole class, three of them were first years and snickered as they saw Zane and Gliss holding hands. Gliss let go of Zane's hand and slid out her notepad, Zane sighed and pulled his notepad out. The clicking of high heels on polished cement demanded the attention of everyone in the classroom. All eyes drew towards the familiar sound. Mrs McCoy rounded the doorway and stepped into the classroom. She placed her hand palm down on a scanner that protruded from the wall next to the door. The door slid closed with a hiss and a voice sounded around the room. "Welcome Mrs McCoy." She nodded and strode to the front of the room.

Mrs McCoy was a short, shrewd woman with short dark hair. Her face was covered in an enormous amount of makeup. She wore a loose-fitting, dazzling blue dress, and her infamous high heels. Zane had never seen anyone wear them as often as Mrs McCoy. Zane didn't really see the point in the silly shoes, and he could only imagine how uncomfortable they would be to wear. He had asked Gliss once how it felt to wear the accessory; she'd frowned and informed him they were simply the worst invention of all time.

"Good morning, class, it is good to see all of you here on time." She gave a steely gaze to one of the girls who sat behind Zane. The girl quailed and sank further into her chair.

"It has come to my attention that two of our students took a tumble down a hill this morning. May I remind all of you to use the designated landing zones, they were built specifically so we can have safe landings."

She glanced towards Zane and Gliss's direction. Zane tried to hide his embarrassment as he had forgotten the school even had landing zones. If Mrs McCoy noticed his embarrassment, she did not show it. Instead, she turned and swiped her hand through the air, activating the holographic board. Twice during the class Gliss dozed off and was woken up by stern words. The remainder of the day was uneventful and Gliss managed to stay awake for the rest of their classes. As they were retrieving their suits to leave for the day, a buzz sounded in the hallway and a voice came online. A soft female voice came through the speakers,

"Glissandra Dunlap and Zane Whitlock, please make your way to the dean's office."

The voice repeated the message two more times before a soft clicking sound indicated the message had ended. Zane looked over at Gliss who gave him a sharp look. The look only furthered his decision ever to call her by her full name. She grabbed his hand tightly before storming off in the direction of the building's offices. Zane's hand was beginning to throb as they reached the cluster of administrative offices, and he winced as Gliss threw open the door. Zane followed close behind her. He marveled at the fury radiating from Gliss and made a mental note to never get on her bad side. She raised her finger in the air, preparing to confront the one who had wronged her by using her full name. She deflated as she recognized the innocent face of her Aunt Margery, who sat staring at the two of them in a comfortable looking roller chair with a contented smile.

"Marge, what are you doing here?" Gliss said exasperated.

"Surprise! I know, I am so excited to work alongside you!" Margery said, her soft red curls bobbing around on her head as she stood and spread her arms out for a hug. Oddly, the hug never came.

"What's the matter, dear? You look unhappy to see me."

"Marge, I go by Gliss not Glissandra," she said in defiance.

Meanwhile, Zane took a peek at his hand which had begun to turn a deep shade of red. Zane tried to gently pull his hand out of the grip but was met with the squeeze tightening in response. He sucked in a sharp breath as he tried to stifle a yelp.

"I didn't think it was that big of a deal!"

Gliss gave Marge one of the most threatening faces that Zane had ever seen. Marge just smiled back at her and articulated each letter as she spelled out Gliss's full name. Zane began to feel tears forming in the corner of his eyes. Seeing his discomfort, Marge looked down at his hand.

"Glissandra, let go of his hand!" Marge shrieked.

Noticing for the first time, Gliss looked down at Zane's purple colored hand. She immediately let go and Zane brought his hand up to his chest, cradling the injured fingers. Gliss embraced Zane and begged for his forgiveness. Zane nodded and patted her gently on the back with his good hand. The hug ended as someone gave a practiced polite cough to get their attention. Gliss, Zane, and Marge all turned to find the dean hovering in his doorway, eyebrows set in a furrow.

"Zane. Gliss. Please come into my office."

It came as a command rather than a suggestion. Neither of them hesitated to quickly file into the room.

Chapter 4

Early Graduation

The large metal door slid closed with a loud hiss, and the hulking figure of the dean stepped into view from behind them. His big feet thumped loudly on the concrete floor as he stepped around the large oak desk. He plopped down in his extra-large chair that was bolted to the ground as if he were afraid it would be moved or stolen from his office. He gestured to the chairs in front of his desk. They sat down.

"Thank you for coming on such short notice. I know that this may come as a shock, but I am glad to have you both here."

The dean was somebody that most people avoided. The few times that Zane had spoken to the man it had left him shaking for the remainder of the day. The dean was by far the largest man Zane had ever seen. He towered well over seven feet tall, and his hands felt more like baseball mitts than they did hands. Muscles rippled through his tight-fitting, pinstriped suit. His eyes were hidden underneath large, bushy eyebrows. Zane thought they were green, but he couldn't be sure he was correct. His jaw line was thick and well pronounced. The top button on his shirt seemed like it would fly off at any moment, especially if the dean flexed the muscles in his neck.

Zane suddenly realized a question had been asked and it looked as if it were directed towards him.

Zane panicked and said, "Yes."

The eyebrows raised slightly and Gliss sharply kicked Zane's shin. The pain brought him back into reality, "Thank you for being so honest with me, it's refreshing." the dean rumbled back.

Gliss eyed him warily and Zane tried to convey a look of confusion which only made her look at him with more scrutiny.

"Well, let's get to the real reason I have called you two in. This may also come to you as a surprise, but you are the top two students in the general studies program." He paused, waiting for their reactions. Zane and Gliss looked at one another and fist bumped.

"Okay, well then, I have some good and bad news for you; the bad news first so we can celebrate afterwards." He clapped his hands together and Zane swallowed hard as the peals of thunder left his ears ringing.

"The bad news; the school board has decided that the General Studies program is rendered nearly useless and the many course studies within the building sit vacant. It was argued that the program is a near total loss."

He paused making sure the two of them were following him. Zane still didn't know how the information was pertinent to him.

The dean continued, "with that being said, they decided to close down many of the programs. You don't have to worry about the teachers, many of them were hired for multiple positions. They will be moving to the other buildings over the summer. The board wanted to close down the whole building, but I argued that this building is still worth something." His eyebrows raised completely revealing hazel-brown eyes that stared directly at them. Zane was dismayed that his original guess had been wrong.

"Now for the good news; I made a deal with the board. It involves both of you." The dean paused then yelled for Margery to come in. A moment later she appeared holding two black leather folders, with real papers attached to the inside. She handed them to the dean then gave a brief smile before exiting. The dean opened the folders and read the texts contained within. He opened a drawer and lifted a thick pen from the inside. He signed the papers, then placed it back in the desk. The dean slid the leather folders towards the two of them. Zane and Gliss picked up the folders hesitantly. Zane lifted the cover and what he found nearly caused him to fall out of his chair. It was obvious that Gliss was having the same reaction as him because her jaw hung open. Their diplomas laid inside of the folder.

"I do believe congratulations are in order, feel free to hug each other or do whatever it is you youngsters do nowadays."

Gliss leaned over and gave Zane a kiss on the cheek. Zane didn't move from his spot, and the dean interpreted this to be the end of the celebration. He continued.

"The board has issued a challenge for the General Studies building. We have one year to produce a class that will give back to society, the catch being I would have to use students who graduated from the General Studies Program as the teachers for a new course. This will be the part you'll both now play; I need you to help save the building." Zane wanted to hand the diplomas back, grab Gliss and head for home.

"You can count on us, Dean Richardson," Gliss said, giving the giant man a thumbs up.

He beamed. "I can't thank both of you enough for your willingness. We have a faculty meeting first thing tomorrow morning, Marge has your ID badges and paperwork for you to sign outside. You will have until mid-summer to draft your class outline, subject, and a thesis on why you think the program will give back to society or have a positive effect on the community. We are all counting on our brightest students to help us out of this predicament." He smiled and stood up holding out a hand. Zane numbly shook his hand and was slightly aware of his body being pulled from the room. Gliss giddily pulled Zane along then let go and embraced her aunt. The two of them squealed with glee, jumping up and down like schoolgirls. Zane couldn't believe that the display of anger from earlier had been completely resolved.

Marge handed Zane a clipboard, but this time it was virtual. He read through the agreement carefully. When he saw the part about payment, he perked up slightly. The amount seemed generous. Zane wanted to know if it was actually generous or if he was being taken advantage of. So, he whipped out his phone and began to sift through the different answers listed on the internet. The number in the contract seemed to align with what he found. He signed his name on all the places marked with X and handed the pad back to Marge, who looked through the paperwork once more before returning the clipboard back to her desk. She handed Zane his ID badge and gave him a hug. The phone rang and Marge dismissed herself while Gliss pulled Zane from the room.

Once they were out in the hallway, Gliss pulled Zane into a tight hug.

"Zane, I can't believe what just happened to us. This is so exciting! My parents are going to flip."

"I don't believe it either," Zane said looking down at his diploma.

"Isn't this great? We graduated and got jobs the same day! To top it all off, you and I are teaching a class together next year, what do you think our class should be about?" Gliss asked excitedly.

Zane shrugged and absentmindedly answered, "how to disappear, change your identity, move somewhere far away, and start a new life."

Gliss looked at him. "You mean like how to be heroes?"

Zane hadn't thought about it like that. In fact, he thought it was kind of cowardly to run from your problems; those were not the attributes he wanted in a hero. However, Zane thought some of the things could be hero-like, so he said, "sure why not? Either that or we learn how to 3D-print clothing."

Gliss thought about it for a moment.

"I think that's a brilliant idea. The world has been without heroes for too long and it's time they returned."

Zane thought hard about it. He imagined teaching a flock of young fliers like himself how to wiz through the sky and catch falling people or pick up purse-thieves. The more he thought, the more he was beginning to like the idea. A class on heroes and how to be one.

"Gliss, there is just one problem, neither of us knows how to be a hero."

"Well, we have some time to figure that out, plus don't you know the history of every superhero in the past?"

Zane shrugged, embarrassed, "yeah, maybe."

They reached his locker, and he placed his palm on the scanner, the door popped open, and Zane almost left his stack of holographic books inside. He felt weird as he cleared everything out of the locker. They walked towards Gliss's locker to do the same. She did likewise and, as she cleared out the locker, a couple of glass spheres rolled out and fell onto the floor.

Zane knelt down and picked them up, he examined the glass ball. Inside the spheres sat a single piece of glitter. They were different colors and sizes, but each sphere held only a *single piece* of glitter. Zane thought glitter was like rabbits or cockroaches; that there was never just *one*.

Zane held them out to Gliss, who snatched them from him and placed them inside a tube that was concealed in her shoes. Zane couldn't believe he had missed the compartment.

"Before you say anything, I can explain."

Zane let his mouth close, then said, "okay. Let's talk as we fly then."

Zane clipped Gliss in then fell forward, his hands stretched out in front of him. Zane's hands hit the concrete softly and he did a push up, shoving the two of them into the air. Zane turned the dial on his helmet and Gliss began to explain.

"So, you obviously know about the glitter but the who, what, where, and when are still mysteries to you and I will fill those in"

"Gliss, I know the who, and some of the what, I know when I found out about it, so, technically, I know a part of the where, as well."

"Listen smart Alek, do you want me to tell you or not?" she asked, Zane sighed, and she continued.

"It all started when I was ten. It happened during the summer, one day I woke up and I felt bumps in my bed. I was shocked to find little glass spheres with glitter in them. I had no idea what they were or how they had gotten there. I first thought it was my brother, so I gathered up the spheres and put them in his room. That same day our house was filled with glitter from floor to ceiling, nearly suffocating all of us. My parents, for the longest time, thought they belonged to my brother, but eventually the secret came out and revealed me as the culprit. When a sphere is crushed, the piece of glitter inside has a reaction to the air which causes the piece to multiply ten thousand-fold. Those are the small spheres. The large ones can get much bigger." She paused as Zane flew above a flock of ducks migrating south.

"They are so pretty when they fly, aren't they?" Gliss asked.

"Yes, but what do ducks have to do with the glitter?"

"Nothing I thought they were beautiful and that you would think so too," she fired back at him. "Anyway, I guess my body produces the spheres when I get nervous, or angry; pretty much any emotion can produce spheres. They only come out of my feet. I don't even feel it happening. So, the other night my boots filled up and one must have slipped out. Multiple times, actually."

"So that is your power? Glitter?"

"Yeah, pretty lame, huh?"

"Not at all! I think there could be many uses for your power."

"Really? Name one." Gliss said, trying to make Zane see her power the same way she viewed it.

"You could distract a bad guy with a cloud of black glitter, or you could fill a pit with glitter and have villains fall in. I think with some engineering and my 3D printer we could even harness the explosive force as a propulsion system to help you jump long distances. Maybe even to allow you to fly," Zane said excitedly.

Gliss paused, then finally gave into his excitement.

"Zane, you don't think like anybody else I know. There is a reason you were the top of our class."

"What do you mean? You were the top student." Zane replied. Gliss shook her head.

"I took a peek at Marge's computer; you were listed as the number one."

Zane turned the knob on his helmet, as his display lit up signaling a phone call from his mother.

"Hi Mom, what's up?" Zane said greeting his mom

"Honey, is it true?"

"Is what true, Mom?" Zane asked. The speaker began to crackle as she responded.

"Kicked out... Gliss... School..."

Zane smacked the side of his helmet with his palm, the signal strengthened, and his mom's crackling voice disappeared.

"What? Sorry, Mom you were breaking up for a second could you repeat that?"

"I said, is it true that today you and Gliss got kicked out of school for good?"

"No, why would you think that? We didn't get kicked out!"

"Well, that's not what Gliss's mother told me."

"Mom, I will explain when I get home, all right? I have to focus on flying right now."

"Fine. But you better have a winning explanation!" With that his mother hung up. Zane twisted the knob back to common communications with Gliss. She didn't answer for some time and Zane was forced to do another circle around her house before she answered.

"I'm so angry right now I could punch something." She said, "I'll take it you were talking to your mom."

"How did you know?" she asked sarcastically.

"I just got off the phone with my mom. She said that your mom told her we had been kicked out of school."

"Yeah, Marge called my mother to inform her we had been expelled. I'm going to break one of my glass beads in her mouth and watch the glitter shoot out of her nose," Gliss said maniacally.

Zane tried to imagine how that would feel. He wasn't sure whether someone could live through it or not.

"Should I land, or do you want to go get something to eat first and face the wrath later?"

"Nah. We should go share the good news as fast as possible, so we won't be punished for filthy lies."

Zane agreed and began their descent. Air wooshed around them and Zane landed in the front yard, this time with more grace. He unclipped Gliss and together they entered the home.

Four disgruntled parents stood in the living room talking in hushed voices. Zane could see his mother's neat ponytail swaying back and forth as she expressed her opinion to the group.

Zane shot a look at Gliss. The lie had turned into a colossal problem. Zane had only ever seen his parents in the same room as Gliss's one other time. It had ended with him grounded for well over two months. Zane swallowed hard, a floorboard creaked underneath Zane's foot and the hushed conversation came to a stop. Four upset faces turned to look at the two of them. Zane's heart leapt into his throat. Gliss, without saying a word, removed the leather folder and opened it for all to see. Three faces stepped in close trying to make out the words on the page.

"Is this some sort of joke?" Zane's Mom said looking at him

"No, this is real," Zane said, fumbling with his backpack, his hands shaking as he pulled out his own diploma and handed it to his mom. She examined it, with Zane's father reading over her shoulder. Then with a smile his mom embraced him in a tight hug. Zane's dad was close behind, turning the moment into a large group hug. Zane felt proud as congratulations floated around the room. The two graduates were forced together in the center of the room as cameras came out and turned the rest of the night into a photo shoot. They all celebrated by ordering in Chinese food and watching a movie. Neither Zane nor Gliss had told their parents about the new job or the predicament the school was in. For now, it was enough for him to have this moment with those he cared about. The evening finally wound down. Zane and his parents said their goodbyes and his mom drove them all home.

Zane read the clock on his nightstand as he readied himself for bed. The analog numbers read one thirty a.m.. He groaned and set his alarm for the morning. He laid down and began to stare at the ceiling. Zane didn't know the first thing about being a teacher. Maybe he could ask his mom for some pointers. Zane sighed then let himself drift off to sleep.

Chapter 5

New Jobs

Gliss emptied her shoe compartments into the larger storage container. She should have probably done this last night but, after their parents had decided to turn the evening into an all-you-can-eat buffet of Chinese take-out, she was just too full to do anything but fall asleep. She noticed that her shoe compartments were almost completely full. She thought about asking her dad for a set of shoes for particularly exciting or emotional days, but then decided that, since she never knew it would be one of those days until it was over, she would probably be fine with her regular shoes. Besides, the compartments had made her soles rather thick and, despite no one noticing or commenting on them so far, she thought making them any thicker would make it look like she was walking around on stilts. This led to a thought of what Zane would think if her new shoes actually managed to make her taller than him. She could imagine his frustrated little frown but then decided it would be altogether too much to be both more threatening and taller than him.

Gliss pulled on a new band T-shirt and looked in the mirror imagining what Zane would think of this one. On the shirt the word "AMPED" was scrawled across the black fabric in jagged electric letters in all manner of neon colors. It wasn't that Gliss liked the shirts; she did for the most part, but sometimes the real fun part of buying a new shirt was just to get a reaction out of Zane. Although, she would never admit it.

She remembered she was supposed to be going to a collaboration meeting and wondered if she should dress up a little bit. Wearing something a little more grown up would be better since they were so young and were likely in need of any respect others would give them. She finally decided on a plain white button-up shirt and a dark pair of jeans. After all, if she tried hard it would look like… Well, like she tried too hard. Not to mention Zane would never let her hear the end of it.

She headed upstairs where her dad was making pancakes in various shapes.

"Good morning, college grad," he called out. Setting some 'graduation cap' shaped pancakes on the table for her.

"Thanks, Dad, but I'm still full from last night." Gliss smiled at her dad's sweet creations.

"You sure square pancakes aren't enough to tempt you? No? Well, then at least eat some yogurt. After all, you still have all day to plan out what you are going to do with your life."

"All right, but Zane and I already have plans for today. He should be here any minute." Gliss said as she accepted the small cup of yogurt and spoon her father held out to her.

"All right, sounds like fun." He replied, humming softly to himself and taking a bite of the corner of a pancake.

"Where is Mom?"

"She had to head out to work early but she told me to give you an extra hug from her."

Gliss's mom was an attorney and often left for work early to get a head start on her cases. Gliss's brother, Travis, idly wandered out of his bedroom, seeming to be in a daze. All of the hair on the left side of his head was sticking straight up. Not that this wasn't normal. His hair always seemed to be sticking straight up. At one point, Gliss had teased him that his power would need to be the ability to control his hair otherwise it would never fall flat. What wasn't normal was that the hair on the right side had mooshed down in some places, so it kind of zigzagged before it sprung up again.

"Nice bed head," Gliss said with her hand over her mouth. Trying to control her laughter. Gliss's dad turned around with a plate of smiley face pancakes and exclaimed "Great gears!''

This was something he seemed to have picked up from his years in a mechanic shop. But did not say nearly as often now that he worked as an engineer.

Travis zombie groaned and meandered over to the bathroom. The two could tell when he finally reached the bathroom mirror because there was an immediate shout, "Holy frog legs!" which was a strange expression even for him.

Gliss's dad wandered over and said he'd better shower or there would be no way of salvaging his appearance before school. Gliss wished her dad goodbye and received both of her parents' hugs from her father as she heard a knock at the door. She opened the door and offered her father a final goodbye as she slipped on her pink flight suit.

Zane greeted her with a big smile, and she gave him a kiss on the cheek. This led to both of them turning a little red in the face. Gliss strapped in and they took off after a short fall off the front steps.

"Hay Zane?" Gliss called.

"Yeah?"

"What do you think they are going to talk about at today's meeting?"

"Probably just talk about how things are going to change."

"You don't think we were supposed to prepare something for it do you?"

"Of course not. The dean didn't say anything about a speech. He is supposed to be the one telling us stuff."

"Right," Gliss's stomach did a flip. They had talked briefly about what they wanted to teach but the reality of how they would teach it was still completely up in the air. She hoped no one would ask too many probing questions about their plans to save the general studies building. Before she had noticed it, they were already descending. It was nice that the commute was short, but Gliss didn't feel all too prepared for what was ahead of them.

"Hey Zane."

"mm-hmm??"

"If anyone asks about our plans, I think we should just say that we are working on something instead of unveiling our big master plan."

"What master plan?"

"Exactly."

"All right, but I'm telling you, you are thinking way too hard about this." Zane said this partly just to get rid of his own anxieties. This time Zane managed to find the right landing zone at the school. Gliss soon found herself reuniting with the ground and she heard the faint sounds of Zane unclipping the safety straps. This was the earliest she had ever been. The school seemed so much more mysterious and darker this early in the morning. Zane pulled his helmet off then looked at her awkwardly before stumbling through his question.

"Gliss, where are we going to put our suits and bags?" That was a good question but, unfortunately for Zane, Gliss did not have the answer. Instead, she just did what she normally did.

Gliss grabbed Zane's hand and began towing him into the General Studies building, the door did not open when she pulled on the cold metal handle. For a moment she panicked before Zane stepped up and placed his ID on the scanner. For a second nothing happened. Then the light flashed green, and Zane opened the door for Gliss. She blushed, then stepped into the empty building.

Together they made their way towards the offices. Before they had a chance to open the door into the collaboration room, the door swung out towards them at an incredible speed. Gliss froze as she watched the dean step out of the doorway. Zane did the same and, for a second, they both stared awkwardly at the dean.

"Good morning, Mr Whitlock and Ms Dunlap. I see you are just in time. If you hurry, you will have the first pick of the bagels," he boomed in his thunderous voice. He smiled and stepped aside, allowing access to the room. They slipped past him and entered the room. The lights had been set to dawn and left the space in near total darkness. They felt their way around a central table and picked two chairs next to one another. Gliss watched as Zane made sure the two of them did not sit at any central point around the rectangular table, avoiding the chairs on the ends and even the ones nearing the middle of the long side. Leave it to Zane to mathematically choose the seats to be least noticed.

"Even if there are bagels, good luck finding them," Zane said leaning over to whisper the comment.

"I know right, what do you think the dean was doing here in the dark?" she asked him. The silence was broken by the door opening again. A line of people entered the room, most of whom she recognized and a few she didn't.

"Rrr, leave it to Bob to set the lights. If he were allowed to set the lights for the school I swear the entire light system would be set to midnight," Mr Thorne said grumbling. The others just shuffled in the darkness still bleary-eyed and not caring enough to mumble their agreement.

Gliss was sure she heard a couple sighs of relief as the darkness was met with the hope of a five-minute power nap. She heard Mr Thorne fumbling around the wall next to the door searching for the lighting panel. The room was soon well lit, and some conversations began to take shape. Gliss pushed her head down towards the table and Zane did, likewise, trying to obscure their identities.

The familiar sound of heels clicking on the polished cement was heard outside the door. Zane inwardly groaned. If there was anyone who could pick out people in a crowd it would be Mrs McCoy. She stepped into the room wearing a bright purple dress that fell down to her ankles. She wore hot pink lipstick and had her hair pulled tightly in a bun. She scoured the room with her all-seeing eyes, then she spotted Gliss and Zane. She narrowed her eyes and began to raise the alarm.

"You two! What do you think you are doing here? This meeting is for the staff only." She pointed an accusing finger towards Gliss who, in turn, pulled out her ID badge and waved it towards the short woman. The physical evidence was not enough for Mrs McCoy.

She stalked over to them and snatched the ID from Gliss who stared at Mrs McCoy with threatening eyes.

"Fake! These ID's are fake!" she shrieked. "Up the both of you! I'm sure the dean will want to deal with you both."

Zane stood up but Gliss defiantly sat in her chair challenging the accusation.

"You're just jealous, aren't you, *Jane*?" Gliss said not letting her eyes break contact with her former teacher. There were more than a few hushed gasps.

"Now you've done it," Mrs Felt shuddered from her chair.

"What did you say, Glissandra? You should know when to hold your tongue!" Mrs McCoy hissed back. Like a hero swooping in at the last second to save a bystander from a bomb, the dean walked back into the room.

"Good, I'm glad you're here, Bob. I have apprehended these delinquents for you! I caught them with forged IDs! Obviously, they are after the bagels!" Mrs McCoy said, holding up the ID badge towards the dean. The dean began to laugh. His deep bellows shook the table. He wiped heavy tears from his eyes, giving the audience time to recover from their tinnitus, before explaining the situation.

"Jane, thank you for your diligence, but Zane Whitlock and Gliss Dunlap are our newest teachers. We should welcome them into the faculty because they are doing us a huge favor. They should even have first pick of the bagels, in fact. I guess I really should have sent out an email informing you of this shocking news." All eyes glued themselves to Zane and Gliss. As clever as Zane was, there was no avoiding the attention now. Many hands shot up before the dean even had a chance to take his seat at the head of the table. Gliss knew the questions would be about them. She was correct as the dean explained the situation. Some of the teachers were shocked to find out they didn't have a class to teach any more and that they would be moving to one of the other buildings. Gliss waited for a long time as the dean continued to explain the plan to save the general studies building. Once again, all eyes fell on the two of them. Gliss swallowed hard as Mrs McCoy piped up and directed a question towards her.

"So, what is your grand plan for a new class that will save the building?"

Gliss looked at the Dean who, in turn, stared at Zane who looked back towards Gliss. The stand-off continued until Zane spoke.

"Well, we have until mid-summer to come up with our idea... We have been giving this a lot of thought, don't worry you can count on us," Zane finished.

"Really? That's the best you've got. Well, I may as well pack up my things now and find a new job. If it were up to me, I would have already drafted up several ideas and lesson plans on how to teach the new class," Mrs McCoy said heatedly.

"Honestly, leaving this up to children and, I mean no offense, who haven't even graduated yet seems a little far-fetched," Mr Thorne said, gesturing towards Zane and Gliss. Continuing he said, "we need someone there who is an adult to make sure the program doesn't fail."

"Silence!" came the shout from the Dean who brought his hand down on the table, cracking the thick wood slab right down the middle. The room fell into a terrible stillness; not even the pitter-patter of a mouse running across the floor would go unheard.

"You don't think I haven't thought about this? The council was adamant. No existing faculty or teachers from other universities are allowed. I know there will need to be an adult involved, so I asked the council if they would allow one to help. They agreed that only an adult who had graduated the General Studies program may be used to help the students focus and develop a plan. That is why they will be working directly with my nephew, Zack, who has been teaching people to fly for the past five years but has agreed to come on to help with this project."

Gliss looked over at Zane who perked up at the mention of the name. Last that she had checked, neither of them knew any relatives of the dean.

The meeting ended early with the now timid teachers scurrying from the room. They avoided Gliss, who tried to smile as they walked by. Mrs McCoy hovered around the far end of the room. Gliss thought the moment would have been better if a rain cloud appeared over her former teacher's head and began dumping buckets of rain on her. The thought made her smile, and she wished the phenomenon would actually happen. To her annoyance, it did not and, like a pest, Mrs Mccoy waited until the opportune time to strike. The moment presented itself when the only ones who remained in the room were Zane, the dean, Gliss, and Mrs McCoy. She didn't waste a second as she slammed the door closed and strode over to the dean, who in turn gave her an icy stare.

"Robert, you have a decision to make, either these two are fired immediately or I will quit. You're not beyond reason yet, are you? Be rational, let me pick the students to save the program; we all know that you lack vision."

"Jane, pack your things, you can leave. No one, I mean no one, tells me I lack vision. I've only dreamed of saying this. You're fired." Zane and Gliss watched the exchange in total silence. Mrs McCoy stormed out of the room leaving the three of them standing in awe. Gliss had never expected this; Mrs McCoy was rude, mean, unwavering, but Gliss didn't feel that she deserved to be fired. She also didn't feel like poking the bear. Maybe she could talk with the Dean later.

"Well, I have sent Zack your phone numbers and he will be in contact with you soon. Let's get working on this. Also, Ms Dunlap could you fill in teaching Mrs McCoys classes for today? It will be good for you to learn how to handle teaching students."

Gliss swallowed hard and gave the dean a thumbs up. Zane mumbled something about using the bathroom and left the room. Gliss ended up alone walking down the halls towards her former teacher's classroom. The rest of the day flew by in a daze and Gliss let the majority of the classes watch a movie of their choosing. Zane tried to swing by for lunch to talk with her, but Gliss didn't feel like talking and brushed him off. She couldn't shake the feeling something was going to go horribly wrong with the next year. She caught a cab home and locked herself in her room for the rest of the evening. She didn't even let her parents enter her room when they knocked; she just turned up her music louder.

Chapter 6

Did Somebody Say Attack?

Zane couldn't figure out why Gliss had turned him down for lunch and refused to let him fly her home. Maybe it was the lingering scent of the cologne. Maybe it was the fact he had forgotten to brush his teeth that morning. Either way it was definitely his fault and he needed to fix it. Zane was about to ask his mom for advice, but his dad walked in the living room instead and asked him how his day had been. Zane sat back on the leather couch and prepared for the conversation to naturally ensue.

"Good, I guess I never told you about why Gliss and I graduated early did I?" His dad handed him a glass of lemonade and sat down across from him.

"No, you didn't, is it a good story?"

"Well, it is all pretty odd, that's for sure," Zane said before taking a long sip from the sweet, refreshing lemonade.

"I can't wait to hear it; should we get your mother for this? She hates it when we leave her out of things." Zane nodded and together with his father they began to yell. His dad acted as if he had been stabbed and even went as far to roll onto the floor, spilling lemonade all over the hardwood.

"All right. All right, I'm coming," his mother's voice said, from the next room.

When she entered, she gave an exaggerated gasp and in a false voice said, "Oh no, darling, did Zane poison you? Or was it my toxic point of view?"

The three of them burst out laughing and Zane found himself feeling much better as the three of them cleaned up the spilled drink. Once they were all settled, Zane began to explain the reason for his early graduation. "So, we have to save the school," Zane finished. He looked at his parents, who sat staring at him in disbelief. Zane's mom had to make sure that Zane was being honest, so she immediately dialed up her best friend. A moment later, Zane could hear Gliss's mom's voice come online. His mom took the call into the other room and Zane's dad was examining the faculty ID; he flipped it over in his hand and read the numbers on the back. He let out a low whistle and congratulated him.

"I'm proud of you, son. Does this mean you're going to move out this summer? I mean you're going to be eighteen in a couple weeks." The comment caught Zane off-guard as he had never given any thought to moving out. Why would he? After all he was an only child, and he didn't think he took up too much space.

"I never thought about moving out. Is there a reason I should?" Zane asked his father while looking him directly in the eyes ensuring that he would get a straight answer out of him.

"Dang it, Zane, why do you have to look at me like that?" he sighed before continuing.

"Well, your mother and I were going to wait until you graduated to tell you, but you've already done that. Zane, your mother and I are going to sell our house and move into a smaller place closer to Korish. It will be closer to the college your mother works at, so she won't have as long of a commute. Plus, the market right now is really good." Zane couldn't believe the words he was hearing coming from his father's mouth.

"You were going to wait to tell me this? Really Dad? This has been our home... well, forever. We can't sell our house."

"You're too late, Zane. Your mother and I have already decided this is going to happen. I was going to tell you soon; don't worry, we will help you find somewhere to live. You can come visit anytime you want."

Zane groaned. He would have to wait to ask his parents about Gliss. Zane had more than enough on his plate. He gave his dad a hug, then walked down the hallway and up the stairs to his room. He looked around at his meager belongings and began to put them in the center of the room. The pile was mostly composed of clothes, but he had a couple of action figures poking out from places within the pile. At least the move into his new place would be easy. Zane could fly his entire life's belongings over in a single duffle bag.

Zane flopped onto his bed and pulled out his phone. He opened his contacts and easily found Gliss's phone number. He tapped the contact and her face appeared. He tapped the number a second time and the phone began to ring. The call rang through and the familiar sound of Gliss's voicemail appeared over the line.

"Hello, you have reached Gliss. I'm sorry I couldn't take your call; I'm probably out kicking butt or something amazing. Don't leave me a message because I won't listen to it. See ya!"

The call ended and Zane exhaled. Before he put his phone on the charger, it began to buzz in his hand. Zane didn't recognize the number, but he swiped the green button, answering the call.

"Hey, bro, is this Zane…?" There was a slight pause as Zack was obviously reading his last name from a paper, "Whitlock?"

"Yes, this is him," Zane answered

"Cool, your name sounds familiar, man. Have we met before?"

"I think so, you gave me my flying test last week."

"Oh yeah. You're the kid who couldn't fly fast right?"

Zane was hoping he had forgotten that part. "Yeah that's me," Zane said sheepishly.

"Cool, did my uncle tell you I will be helping teach your class next year?"

"Yep"

"Cool, well, do you mind if we meet up some time to go over the game plan?"

"Nope, I don't mind."

"Could you tell that girl too; She didn't answer my phone calls."

"Sure, I can tell her"

"Sweet, we can meet at my uncle's place. I'm kind of between apartments right now and looking for a roommate. I will text you his address."

"All right sounds good. You said next week, right?" Zack laughed.

"How about in two hours we meet. The sooner the better right?" Zane laughed but agreed to the plan. The phone call ended and a moment later a text came through with an address. Zane saved the information to his device and pulled himself from his bed. Maybe he could get an apartment with Zack. It seemed like a good idea.

Zane put on his suit, snuck out his window, and fell towards the ground. Then began to hover and headed towards Gliss's. It was late and he was sure she would have finished dinner by now. Zane plugged in the address and turned on some music as he flew. The familiar beat and lyrics took his mind off of things, and he found himself in a better mood as he descended towards Gliss's house. Zane walked up to the front door and pushed the button on the doorbell. Feet scurried in the house hidden by the front door, the knob jiggled, and the door opened, revealing Travis, who beamed as he saw Zane.

"Welcome to our humble abode," he said with a slight bow feigning formality. He lost his composure as Zane entered the home and began to laugh.

"Hey, Travis. It's good to see you. Still killing it with the ladies?" Zane asked, teasing his friend. Travis accepted the compliment and smoothly slid his hand over the top of his hair slicking it back. He gave Zane two finger guns and clicked with his tongue before saying, "You know it."

Zane laughed and together they found their way into the kitchen. "So, where is your sister?"

"You can't hear? She locked herself in her room and won't come out. Mom and dad have been down there for hours trying to get her to talk," he said.

"Oh," Zane replied. He started rethinking his decision to come over and get Gliss for the meeting with Zack. Maybe he should go alone to the first one.

"She might come out to see you though; I know it would make mom happy. She has been having a rough week, ever since the dishwasher went out."

Zane smiled at Travis and decided the risk was worth it. He gathered all the courage he could muster together and walked down into the basement. Zane almost walked back up as he saw Mr and Mrs Dunlap on the ground literally begging at the foot of Gliss's door. The door was vibrating, and Zane could hear the angsty teen music coming from within the door's confines. Zane cleared his throat.

"Oh, Zane thank you for coming so quickly! We have tried everything to get her to listen. I'm glad you listen to your mother; unlike someone we know." Mrs Dunlap said, elevating her voice at the last part.

"Yes, thank you for coming, I'll get her to turn down the music so you two can talk." Mr Dunlap said, walking over to a circuit breaker panel on the wall. He opened the case and pulled a lever. A second later the basement was cast into darkness, and the music ended abruptly. Mrs Dunlap ran over cowering behind her husband. They both ushered Zane to walk towards the door. Zane did not want to but with the help of Travis he found himself standing inches away. Zane swallowed hard. He could hear Gliss preparing herself to explode. He heard her breaths coming in quicker and quicker. A guttural sound began to form at the back of her throat, and she was beginning to produce a monstrous roar. The door flew open, and the scream came out. Zane winced and backed away. Gliss's face was a brilliant red, her eyes were black and filled with hate. Zane had never seen her like this before.

"Retreat!" cried Travis. Zane could hear three pairs of feet pounding up the stairs. Recognition flashed in her eyes, but Zane stumbled back away from her.

"Zane, I thought that, of all people, you could respect my privacy." Zane looked around; the rest of the household had exited the blast radius.

"Hey, Gliss, you look great!" Zane tried, thinking that a compliment would be the correct approach for the situation at hand. He was wrong. Nothing would have been a correct response., Gliss reached a hand in her pocket and hurled a glass sphere at Zane. The small bead- like object hit him hard in one shoulder and Zane heard the now familiar sound of breaking glass, He sucked in a mouthful of air before his body was tossed backwards from the multiplying glitter explosion. A second sphere caught him right below his left eye, it broke on his skin and Zane was lucky enough to brush it off his face, before he lost his head. Black and crimson glitter filled the air along with a torrent of obscenities coming from Gliss. Zane didn't even know what some of them were. He searched around in the glitter-filled air for an escape and caught a glimpse of light shining down from the stairs. Zane ran and tore up the stairs. As he reached the top, three grinning faces closed the landing's door, trapping him in the basement. Zane still clutched his helmet in one hand, his lungs were burning, begging for air. He pulled the helmet on and activated the interface. The helmet sealed and fresh air filtered in through the ventilation system. Maniacal laughter sounded around him, and Zane began to panic.

"Gliss, I'm sorry. Please don't do anything you will regret, all right?" Zane yelled down the stairs. A third glass sphere came as a response. It broke behind Zane and the resounding explosion of deep green glitter shoved him down the stairs. His instincts kicked in and Zane found himself floating near the basement floor..

"How should we settle this?" said Gliss who still was invisible to Zane. He searched the space frantically for a means of escape. There were no windows. His only exit had been cut off by traitors.

"Maybe by talking about our feelings instead of trying to kill me," Zane yelled.

"Sounds pretty lame to me. How about we fight to the death?" came the reply. Zane saw a flash of movement and sped towards it. Two spheres caught him in mid-flight; the first one sent him shooting upwards. He skidded along the ceiling while dark orange glitter spewed from beneath him. Just as he thought the ride was over, the second sphere's integrity gave out and Zane shot to the right in a dizzying spiral. He hit the floor and lay still, trying to keep his dinner down. Zane didn't move a muscle and he didn't respond when Gliss began to taunt him.

"Oh, is the poor little Zane going to be all right? Where did he go? Did he get hurt?" She paused and Zane held his breath, his heart was pounding so loud he was sure anyone within ten feet of him could hear it. Mr Dunlap called down the stairs from his safe, elevated position, "Gliss, sweety, don't hurt anyone. We were the ones who put Zane up to this." If Gliss heard her father she decided not to respond. Zane waited for a couple minutes longer and the Gliss he knew returned, replacing the scary one.

"Zane, seriously are you okay? I can't find you anywhere." Zane let out a sigh of relief but decided to dish out some payback, so he let out a soft groan, then positioned one leg underneath him uncomfortably. A moment later Gliss was by his side scooping handfuls of glitter off his body. She tried to ask him questions, but Zane acted like he was in a daze. He watched as she reached down to remove his helmet.

"Zane… Zane are you all right?" She tugged on the helmet and, as it slid off Zane let out a scream so perfect, he even surprised himself. Gliss began to scream with him, and Zane couldn't keep a straight face any longer. His scream soon turned into uncontrollable laughter. Gliss looked down at him with disgust. Zane would have described it as loving disgust, if that were even a thing. She dropped his helmet onto his chest and stalked away.

"Gliss, where are you going?" Zane called after her. "To my room."

"Wait, don't leave me out here all alone. We have a meeting in like ten minutes." Gliss stopped in her tracks. They were quite visible even in the darkness.

"What are you talking about? We don't have a meeting."

"Check your messages. Zack, the dean's nephew, set up a meeting for tonight."

Gliss pulled out her phone, opened the main screen and her face registered shock. "Wow, thirteen missed calls, seven text messages. And those are only the ones from your mom." Gliss exclaimed.

"Yeah, we better get going if we're going to make it," Zane said while rising from the depths of the glitter pool.

"Sorry for earlier. I guess that I just had a difficult day."

"I understand. If something is bothering you, then you should just tell me instead of trying to kill me."

"Well, someone has to give you practice at beating villains. I can be a pretty good bad guy. Speaking of which, you sucked at being a hero. I totally won," she said making her way over to the panel on the wall. She easily pulled the lever and the lights flickered on. Zane cringed as he noticed the damaged drywall on the ceiling.

"I was holding back because I didn't want to hurt you. Also, being a good bad guy is an oxymoron and I didn't suck, I 'flew it' at being a hero.," Zane finally said in response, hoping his pun was light. Gliss shrugged, then took his hand and led him over to an enormous fan. She flipped the switch at its base and Zane gripped her hand tighter as the blades began to pick up speed. Soon large spirals of glitter began to blow around the room. There was a sucking noise that sounded from somewhere in the back wall. Zane was amazed as he turned around inspecting the basement; all the glitter was gone. Gliss smiled then noticed the ceiling. She gasped then whispered,

"I won't tell him if you won't."

"I am pretty sure your mom already knows," Zane responded.

"Curse her sixth sense! You are right," Gliss said.

She shrugged and together they headed up the stairs. Gliss gave three distinct knocks and locks began to slide on the opposite side of the door. Travis was the first one to peer through at them. He pulled his head back and whispered something to his parents. The door swung all the way open and soon Gliss and Zane were pulled into a giant group hug.

The hug ended and, without telling her parents too much information about the meeting, Zane and Gliss were permitted to leave the house. It was only under a strict promise to feed Gliss and have her home before midnight that they were able to leave.

Zane and Gliss flew through the city, heading for their destination. Little did they know that somebody was watching their every move.

Chapter 7

Planning Meeting.

Zane and Gliss touched down at the dean's house. Zane gulped as he was unaccustomed to seeing teachers off the clock. It was always awkward when he saw them in stores over the summer. Gliss tried to step away from Zane and nearly pulled him over.

"Aren't you going to unhook me?" she asked impatiently. All her former animosity for the day had vanished and Zane was happy to see her in such a good mood.

"Sorry, I was lost in thought."

"It better have been a big thought to get lost in."

Zane chuckled at the comment. He loved how she was so witty.

"I wish I could tell you it was a good one, but I can't with an honest conscience," Zane said while unhooking the safety straps. Gliss turned and gave him a smile then leaned in to give him a quick kiss. Zane relaxed as he enjoyed the moment and wished it wouldn't end. Like snow melting under the warmth of a spring sun, the moment ended. The doorbell rang moments later and the two of them stood waiting for the answer. The front porch shuddered as thundering steps neared the entry, Dean Richardson stepped out joining the two of them in the cold night wearing black sweatpants and a tight purple shirt.

"Can I help you two?" the dean said, his eyebrow furrowing.

"We are here for a meeting with Zack," Zane replied.

"Oh well, in that case, come on in," the dean said gesturing with a mammoth hand. Gliss and Zane stepped into the home which was less spectacular than he had imagined. All the walls and floors were made of concrete. Even colored concrete still didn't feel cozy. If there were doors leading into any rooms, they were made of dark heavy steel. All the chairs were fashioned out of metal and were bolted to the floor.

Zane found himself wondering what kind of power the dean possessed. The door closed hard behind them and Gliss flinched slightly.

"Zack ,you have company," the dean boomed. Zane and Gliss waited for what seemed like an obscene amount of time before Zack came meandering down the hallway into the front room.

"Bro! it's totally you." he said, finally taking a moment to look up from his phone screen. Zack looked totally different than Zane thought, as he had appeared different in his flight suit.

Zack had long brown hair that seemed to clump together in tubelike tendrils and orange eyes which Zane didn't think looked natural. Zane had never actually seen anyone with the eye color. Zack was skinny and wore a shirt with the arm sleeves cut off. His jeans looked so tight that they would restrict any movement.

"I thought you would be nerdier though. Maybe a pair of glasses or something like that." Zack said before Zane could respond.

"Yeah, and you look different than what I thought," Zane blurted out.

"You honestly thought that I would be a clean-cut guy wearing a suit and carrying a briefcase?"

"No… I just didn't expect…"

Zane reached up to his own head and Zack finished the sentence.

"Hair. I know. It's rad, right? It's taken me longer than I would like to admit but I think it is coming along great."

Zack turned looking at his uncle waiting for praise that did not come instead Dean Richardson just grumbled.

"Come on in, I have some paper and stuff for our meeting." Zack said, waving over his shoulder for the two of them to follow. Zane thought it was just going to be the three of them in the meeting.

He felt uncomfortable as the dean sat cross-legged on the opposite side of the room from him on the concrete floor. It looked as if the pose was causing some discomfort to the hulking man. When Zane suggested they pull in some chairs he saw fear flash briefly on the dean's face.

Zack was the first to shoot down the idea saying that the hard floor was a good way to keep them awake and focused. Zack pulled out a big box and removed sheets of paper, pens, pencils, and erasers. Gliss was the first one to snatch up a pen. She examined it with awe. Zane pulled a sheet of paper from the stack and rubbed it between his fingers. There was something about it that he found extremely pleasant.

"Where did you get all this?" Gliss asked, testing the pen tip on her hand.

"Well, the paper I make myself. I even grew the trees. The pens, pencils and erasers I ordered online from a specialty store in Romania," Zack answered.

"So, do you have any ideas for the class?" Zane looked at Gliss.

She stared back at him then said,

"Well, we have only had one idea and it was to teach a class on how to be heroes," Gliss said looking at her feet as she caught the gaze of the dean.

"No way! I was totally thinking the same thing! You're not a mind reader, are you?" Zack asked Gliss

"No, this was as much my idea as it was Zane's. Plus, he knows more about superheroes than anyone I have ever met," she said in a matter-of-fact way.

Zane looked at the dean who just sat looking as uncomfortable as he had earlier. A few more questions were asked about the curriculum, classes, and needs the classroom would have. The ideas flowed and the papers began to be filled with handwriting. Zane was even surprised when he found the dean had filled out perhaps more paper than anybody else in the room. "Dean, are you allowed to give any input, or will the council get angry that you helped?" Zane asked.

"Why wouldn't I be allowed to give my input? I mean, the decision is yours on what you submit to the council. I don't know whether they will go for the hero idea or not. They might think it will fail and still give the approval or they could decline it because they wouldn't want bad publicity for the school if something were to go wrong," He paused, looking at the occupants of the room. All eyes were on him.

"Well, what do you think about it?" Gliss asked

"I actually think that it is a brilliant idea. The position we are in as a school needs something bold; something that hasn't been done before. Or at least in a very long time. If you get the approval then you will have to fill out a lot of paperwork, you will have to get all your students to pass the hero exams and to get work release forms into the school and city. I mean what you are talking about doing would be a lot of work. If I could make a suggestion. If it were me, I would get a list of students who are going to be registered in your class next year and get a head start on all the paperwork. I would visit them in person to get all the forms out of the way before the school year begins." Zane was scribbling furiously on his paper trying to write down all the different things the dean had suggested. Zack lay back on the floor and dismissed the meeting.

The dean looked relieved as he stood up He walked them to the door and, together, Zane and Gliss exited the house.

"Zane?"

"Yeah, Gliss?"

"How do you think the dean knows so much about the paperwork involved with becoming a registered hero?"

Zane hadn't thought about it.

"Maybe he has had experience helping students in the past with it," Zane answered, as he fell off the front steps.

"Did you see how he was scared when you mentioned bringing chairs in?"

"Yeah, I did. I thought it was kind of odd."

"Do you think the dean is a hero and that is why he knows about the paperwork?"

Zane paused, thinking about the question; it was a possibility. The problem was Zane didn't know enough about the dean's abilities, other than his incredible strength and the odd fear of chairs.

"Zane?" Gliss asked, waiting impatiently for his response.

"Sorry, I don't know, Gliss, he could be. There were only a few heroes with super-strength, and they left a while ago, but the dean would have to be really old to fit the bill. Ever since the powers got 'weaker,' there isn't anybody who would match his description. Anyway, where do you want to go for dinner?" he asked, while looking at the clock in his helmet. They had spent two hours at the dean's house planning.

"How about Jan's Cafe?" came the reply.

"Sounds good to me," Zane turned the knob on the side of his helmet so he could deliver the set of commands to set Jan's as their destination.

The arrows projected out in front of him a moment later and he decided to leave the communications off for a minute longer so he could think. Zane looked down at the lights that littered the ground below him. He did his checks on his radar and other diagnostics, making sure they were not in any danger. The suit confirmed their flight would be safe. Zane wished he could just fly all the time as he loved the feeling of freedom. Zane felt comfort from his power. It always gave him another option. He could just forget his problems and fly far away from them. He finally turned the knob back on as he noticed the blue indicator in the corner of his helmet.

"Did you get lost in another thought?" Gliss asked sharply.

"Yeah, sorry," Zane apologized

"Well, maybe if you thought more about me than other boring things then you wouldn't forget about me."

Zane laughed, which only urged her to continue. The two of them went back and forth with one another until they landed gently outside Jan's Cafe. They pulled off their helmets and headed inside the small building.

The two of them had been coming to Jan's Cafe as long as they could remember. They loved it, despite its many flaws. The building was outdated, bricks crumbling at the corners, the paint was faded, and the parking lot was full of potholes. The interior had fared just as badly; with menus that were made of a composite sticky rubber, the booths had rips in the upholstery and the salt and pepper shakers' lids did not stay on all the time. The last problem had given cause for a fun game they had invented; they would take three salt shakers and play a game of rock paper scissors to determine which one they and their family members would use for the duration of the visit.

It had ended many times with mouths dry and salty.

They walked in the main door and a bell chimed informing the waitress of their presence.
"Welcome to Jan's Cafe. Choose any seat you would like." Jan said waving at the two of them without looking up. Jan was an elderly woman. She had a smile that could melt away the coldest of days. Her eyes were a deep mysterious brown, and her hair was kept loose and fell around her shoulders in large swooping black curls.

"Hi Jan, it's good to see you," Gliss said in a bubbly friendly tone. Jan looked away from the book she was reading, and a smile spread across her face.

"Well, if it isn't my two favorite customers, Gliss and Zane. How are your moms doing?"

"Thanks, Jan, they are doing good," Zane said and Gliss nodded her head in agreement.

"Well, good, what brings you in on this fine night? Any special occasions to celebrate?"

"Now that you mention it, yes, there have been quite a few things to celebrate."

Gliss began to tell Jan everything that had happened recently. She told her about Zane getting his flyer's license, about the two of them graduating early and landing new jobs, then finished off by informing Jan that Zane and herself were now dating.

"Well, I'll be. I just knew that you two would eventually find each other. It sounds like you have been busy with schoolwork and such! I'll tell you what, dinner's on me tonight."

No matter how many times Zane tried to object to the free food, Jan just batted away the comment with a "no, this is my treat, for my two favorite customers."

Zane gave up halfway through the meal and just enjoyed himself. The three of them sat together reminiscing on fun memories that had taken place through the years in the café. They laughed and told stories for what seemed like forever. Zane pulled Gliss from the café and they waved their goodbyes to Jan, who waved and gave them a big smile. Zane took off towards the skies. He didn't realize he had done it until Gliss's voice came thundering in from the headset. Zane nearly took them for a dive at the sudden sound.

"Zane, did you just take off without falling?" Gliss asked in an excited voice.

"I…" Zane paused, trying to recall the take-off. The memory was foggy. All he remembered was taking off, Jan's smile and the warmth he felt from it then he had flown. Zane couldn't believe it himself; He had actually taken off from the ground without tripping.

"I did, I don't know how I did it, but I did," Zane said, with excitement. With a loud, "WOOHOO!" Zane did a large loop in the sky. Gliss laughed. Zane's excitement ended as his display began to blink and he answered the phone call from Gliss's father.

"Where in the blasted world are you? We had an agreement, Zane." For the first time Zane noted the analog clock in his display. 1:23a.m. Zane groaned inside.

"Sorry, Mr Dunlap, I lost track of time."

"If you keep track of my daughter like you do time then you might lose her too. Get her home in the next fifteen minutes or you won't be seeing Gliss for the rest of the summer," he said sternly into the phone. Before Zane had the chance to respond, the line cut out, leaving Zane with his mouth open. Gliss's voice came on moments later,

"Uh... Zane, I think you might want to get me home soon..." Gliss said, genuine worry in her voice.

"Yeah, your dad just informed me of that."

"He told you that my mom was on her way to my room to sell my extremely rare, vintage stereo?"

"No, he said I have to get you home in the next fifteen minutes or else I won't be able to see you until the end of summer."

"Who cares about empty threats, Zane... When my mom promises to do something, she will actually do it."

Zane flew as fast as his body would allow towards Gliss's home. He arrived sixteen minutes later. He unhooked Gliss and she threw open the front door and charged down the stairs. Gliss's father stepped outside joining Zane on the front porch. Zane backed away from him, making sure he had the distance he required for a quick get-away.

"Hello, Mr Dunlap. I am sorry for getting Gliss home so late."

"You can call me, Dale. I was just trying to get you home before Denise actually posted Gliss's stuff for sale online. I don't think Travis and I would survive a war between the two of them." Zane relaxed when he realized that Dale wasn't angry at him.

"So, how did the meeting go?"

"Good, I guess. It sounds like a lot of work."

"Well, all good things come from a lot of work."

"Yeah, I guess they do."

"So, what was this meeting for? Was it a job interview?" It was at that moment Zane realized Gliss still hadn't told her parents about their jobs. He didn't feel like it was his obligation.

"Not exactly. But it was for our new jobs. I'm sure Gliss can fill you in on the rest."

Dale eyed him but shrugged and let Zane go home. Zane snuck into his bedroom, exhausted. The day had been long and eventful. Zane collapsed on his bed and fell asleep.

Chapter 8

Not Summer Vacation

Summer was now in full swing, and Zane had never not enjoyed a summer so much in his life. This had been the most exhausting, sleepless, paper-filled summer he had ever lived through. He let his legs dangle off the edge of his bed. Moving in with Zack had not been as exciting or as fun as he had first thought it would be. Zane appreciated his mother more and more every day as he watched piles of dishes, clothes and an assortment of empty cans, bags, and wrappers accumulate on the ground. It was getting to the point that when Zane got up in the night to use the bathroom he was tripping and falling over traps set by himself.

A shriek from the living room told him that Gliss had dropped by for a visit. Zane peeled himself from his bed, his hair felt like it was going to be extra unruly today.

"Ew, ew, this is so gross!"

Zane found Gliss standing a couple feet away from the front of the sink that was overflowing with dishes. " Hey, Gliss, how's it hanging?" Zack said, emerging from the depths of a pile of dirty laundry. She yelped as clothes dripped and oozed off Zack. He looked like some kind of monster.

"Good morning, Gliss," Zane said. She turned at him then in her most motherly voice began to tell him that he was, in simple terms, a slob.

"Zane, I will not go on another date with you until this place is spotless," she said, exiting the apartment. Zane followed her out into the hallway.

"Gliss, stop," he called after her. She turned to face him, then pointed at a sock that had attached itself with some chewing gum to his shirt. Zane watched the gooey tendrils stretch as he removed the sock from his shirt.

"Gliss, come on, don't go. We have the board review today and we need to go over notes."

"Not a chance, you have one hour to meet me at my house looking and smelling presentable." With that she walked down the hallway, then rounded the corner heading towards the stairs. Zane walked back into the apartment. Zack had disappeared once again into the pile of clothes. It's not that Zane was a particularly dirty individual; it was the simple fact he had been hard-pressed for time and was struggling to find a healthy balance. Gliss still had her mother who wouldn't let her leave the house if her bed wasn't made. Once Zane had moved out and in with Zack, he had been forced to learn how to cook, pay rent, and live with somebody he hardly knew.

Zane sighed at the untidy space, then he set to work cleaning. An hour later, he was wearing a hand-washed shirt and a pair of jeans he had found at the bottom of his suitcase. The rest of the apartment, aside from the dishes and stack of trash bags in the living room, was once again a livable space. Zane threw on some deodorant, brushed his teeth for the first time in two weeks, and combed his hair. He ran out the door and caught a glimpse of Zack staring at the now-clean apartment in a reverent kind of way. He didn't have time to say anything to Zack, so he pulled his helmet on and did a swan dive off the balcony.

Zane's body rushed towards the ground before it streaked away in a burst of motion. He clipped the tops of the high-cut grass. Zane began a steady incline and checked his radars and the chatter. It had taken a couple of weeks for him to be able to fly to Gliss's house without his GPS guidance system. He found the challenge thrilling. Zane flew through the hot summer air, watching the airplanes and other people flying on the international flyway above him. Some of them flew at incredible speeds. Zane had tried to fly up there once with Zack; they had taken an emergency exit because Zane couldn't get up to speed. He had blamed it on being nervous and Zack had never pressured him into flying on the flyway again. But Zane knew that it wasn't because he had been nervous. There was something inside of him that wouldn't let him go fast. He wished he knew what the block was. For now, Zane kept to the low altitudes.

He spotted the familiar configuration of buildings that indicated he was coming up to Gliss's. He began to dive, picking up speed. Zane landed a little harder than he intended on Gliss's roof. He even found himself performing a somersault coming to rest on one knee. He hoped that no one had heard him land.

Gliss had come up with the idea to trade off practicing to be a villain for a week at a time, while the others tried to practice the hero tricks they had been studying over the summer. It was Zane's turn to be the hero, so he jumped into the air then hovered only inches from the shingled roof. Zane moved silently over to one side of the house. He peered over the side, gazing into a window. The room seemed to be empty. So, he lowered himself down in front of the window. Zane removed the window screen, then tried the window and it slid open easily. Zane floated inside the room; it looked different than he remembered. The kitchen was entirely different; the cabinets were a deep red and the countertops a brilliant white polished marble. Zane slid the window closed behind him.

He knew that the Dunlaps were always changing things and dismissed the different kitchen layout. Zane began to circle the front room when he looked out the window and across the yard to the house next door. There across the yard, he saw Gliss and Travis through the window. They were talking to their mom. Zane went pale as he heard footsteps coming up from the basement. Zane flew to the front door and tried the handle. Alarms began to sound as the door was pushed open. Shouts came from behind him.

"Stop, you thief!"

Zane didn't wait around to see what happened next, instead he took off across the lawn. The thought hit him that if he ran to Gliss's house then she would find out about his escapade through her neighbor's house and so would the neighbor. So, Zane flew by her window and locked eyes with her as he took to the sky. He wasn't sure she knew exactly what the stare meant. He wasn't sure what it meant. So, he soared upwards. Shouts continued to be hurled at him from the chunky man in the bathrobe who was now shaking a fist at Zane.

Zane waved to the man and circled the area. He headed towards his childhood house. He landed outside and stared at the house. He sighed then started walking towards Gliss's house. When he was sure he was the only one on the street, he stepped behind a tree and took off his flight suit. Zane stuffed the helmet and suit in his backpack. The walk took him a little longer than he remembered. When Zane arrived, police cars were lined up outside Gliss's neighbor's house. Zane shielded his face as he walked up Gliss's front steps. He knocked on the door and Gliss pulled him into the living room. She closed the blinds nearest them.

"What did you do?" she asked in a hushed voice. Zane didn't want to answer her honestly, but it was the only explanation that made sense.

"I thought that it was your house, so I snuck in because it is my turn to be the hero," Zane replied.

Gliss could not contain the laughter that spilled out from her. She laughed until large tears dripped down the sides of her cheeks. Zane wanted to hide.

"Zane, did you hear that someone broke into Mr Wilson's home?" Denise asked as she walked into the front room. Zane laughed nervously,

"Yeah, Gliss, was just telling me."

"So crazy! In broad daylight and in our neighborhood too." She shook her head then walked over to Zane and straightened the collar on his shirt. She patted him on the head and walked back into the kitchen.

"So, are we going to review our notes and thesis?" Zane asked, pulling out paper from his backpack, which was now wrinkled slightly. He smoothed it out over one leg and handed it to her. Gliss read the first line, frowned… read the second line, smiled and handed the papers back to him.

"Zane, I'm sure we don't need to go over it again, plus the meeting is in ten minutes and that is not enough time to even read the introductory statements. Let's get going."

Zane's hands began to tremble slightly as the nervousness set in. "Yeah, you're right, everything's going to go okay, right?" Zane asked.

"Of course, dummy, we are geniuses. How could they reject our idea? The dean even likes it." The words brought him little comfort.

Gliss disappeared downstairs and, a moment later, reappeared wearing her hot pink flight suit. She ran over and grabbed his hand, then noticed that Zane wasn't wearing his. A flicker of understanding resonated in her eyes, and she smiled and tugged him out the door. Zane protested and a strong, armed officer stepped over to greet them.

"Have you two seen anything suspicious going on in the last few hours?"

"As a matter of fact, I have, Officer Denton. I saw a short, fat man come flying out of that house earlier. I didn't get a good look at his face, but he looked middle-aged."

The officer had pulled out his holographic notepad and was scribbling furiously.

"Can I get a name from you to put on this report?"

"Gliss Dunlap."

"Thank you."

Gliss and Zane snuck away and began to walk down the street.

Once they were out of view, Zane hissed, "Gliss, what did you do that for? You just lied to a police officer, that could get you in real trouble." She waved a dismissive hand towards Zane.

"Zane, you're sweet, but Mr Wilson is practically blind. Giving a description that is not you is ensuring your safety and the future of our class."

"Gliss, that's absolutely insane, but thank you for helping me out once again." She leaned in and planted a kiss on his cheek then told him to put on his suit. Zane did as she asked. Once they were strapped in, he fell forward and took off in the direction of the school.

Zane landed and the two of them found Zack lounging around in the grass. He was wearing a black suit and sunglasses with a hat that hid his coiled hair. He had even shaved his stubble. Zack looked perhaps the most presentable out of the three of them. The dean pulled up in his tank of a vehicle. Zane was sure he had seen the car being used in the military. The door popped open, and he stepped out. Zack waved him down and the dean joined them.

He stepped up to the only door that Zane's badge couldn't get him into; it was marked as Council. The light flashed green and together they all stepped in, the dean bringing up the rear. The corridor went on for longer than Zane had imagined. He spent most of the walk trying not to think about the sweat that was pooling in the center of his back and really hoped it wouldn't be visible to the others. The hallway drew to an end and a second metal door stood with a palm and iris scanner set off to one side. The dean had to sneak past them, and he drew more than a few yelps as his feet crushed some toes. The door opened and the group limped into the council room.

Six unfamiliar faces sat at a large table that was positioned on a podium, mostly cast into shadow as a singular light fell upon three chairs that had been set before the main table. The dean made his way up to his chair. There was an audible squeal as the chair protested against the sudden weight.

Zack was the first one to sit, Zane and Gliss followed shortly behind. The room was silent for a few moments before a woman spoke.

"We would like to call this meeting to a start. We will get right to the matter at hand. First ,we will hear the beginning arguments. Those who were asked to prepare, please ready yourselves. Second, we will hear the proposals from the new staff members. They have provided us with the proposed course material and their thesis. To close the meeting, we will vote on how to proceed. Five minutes will be given at the end for questions and answers."

The first lady ended the introduction abruptly and without emotion. She had a business-like way of talking that reminded Zane of a bank teller. She was cut and dry. The dean was the first to give his opening argument. It was the most emotion he had ever seen the large man show. He talked for nearly ten minutes, backing his statements with facts and statistics. Zane was impressed. The dean sat back down and a man from the opposite side of the room stood; his voice was high and shrill but the way he talked was like that of a very educated professor. He gave various scenarios that supported his claims that the General Studies building was becoming obsolete, and the space should be devoted to something more profitable.

Zane felt his blood begin to boil as the man continued to attack the program. He looked over at Gliss, her face was matching her hair in color. Zane knew that if the shrill man didn't finish soon, he was going to get more than an earful from Gliss. An assault charge would most likely be added to the meeting minutes. Zane exhaled as the man finished and sat down.

The lady who began the meeting asked them to bring the papers forward. Zane did as he was asked. He found the blue folder marked 'Class Heroes', pulled it from his phone and placed it on the main computer. It took a moment to upload and soon screens came up in front of all faces present at the meeting.

Zane tried to steady his shaking hand as the faces began to read the proposal before them. Many hands flicked fingers in front of their screens reading the material. Minutes went by before a microphone was passed down to Zack who had been nominated as the speaker for the group. Zane would have nominated Gliss, but he knew that she would find a way to make the arguments come to life and not in a good way. As brilliant as she was, she had shown herself to be a little Hot-headed. When they had practiced giving their speeches, Zane had frozen with just an audience of the dean. He had suggested that Zack be the speaker. He was not their first choice, but it was the best they had. Zack began, "Ladies and Gentlemen of the council, we would like to present to you our proposal to save the General Studies program. Or better yet, save the building and change the program. We have worked tirelessly to bring you what is perhaps the best idea to grace our school's hallways in all its years of service." Zack paused for effect.

"We would like to, with your permission, bring a hero program to the school. Think about the heroes of the past! All the good they accomplished! Remember how close the world was to achieving world peace? We would like to offer students a way to give back to the community by working with local government agencies on small but necessary assignments that would be made easier with superpowers. We would not be like the heroes of old, we would become the heroes of the future, much more efficient; able to work more readily with the government. Our goal is to make it a safer community to live in, to help those in need. You need not worry about our credentials; this summer each of us received our Hero License. We have reached out to community agencies to better understand the role we would take. The agencies that we talked to showed extreme interest in the program. There will be a few hiccups, some things that can't be foreseen. We want to assure you that the program will be in the best hands to bring this new course into the future."

Zack finished and Zane found himself feeling impressed by his colleague. Zack hadn't been their first choice because of his relaxed and unprofessional way of life, but he proved he could put on an amazing façade.

The council woman stepped forward as the microphone retracted from its spot before them.

"Thank you for your presentation. It is time to take the vote. Has everyone reached a consensus?" She turned and looked at the hidden row of shadowed faces. Zane assumed that they all nodded because she continued.

"Well, then, who is in favor of proceeding with the proposed plan?" Five hands raised; they fell. "Congratulations, the motion was passed.

Those who disagree, your votes will be recorded along with your dissenting arguments. Five minutes will be given for questions. Thank you."

The lady returned to her seat and individual microphones rose out in front of each councilperson. The central microphone came back up and a timer was set. Then the questions came. Zane couldn't believe they had done it. He didn't know whether he should feel exhilarated or deflated that the idea had been passed. He had originally hoped that they would shoot the idea down and a different topic would be assigned to them. Zane came back to reality as Gliss nudged him in the side. Zane realized with rising panic that a question had been asked directly to him. "Umm. Sorry, could you repeat the question?"

"I asked, in what ways have you prepared to help your students best succeed in this program when they each have different powers?" an aged man asked, his chin wobbled slightly as he spoke in a near-whisper. Zane took the floor,

"Well, sir, the beauty of the program is the near-infinite need for diverse powers. Each power will be cataloged; that way when we are contacted by local agencies, we can decide who is best suited for the scenario. Each student will have the opportunity to work in everyday situations with those who have been trained to handle the situation placed before them. We will work tirelessly to help each student reach his or her full potential," Zane said, stepping back from the microphone.

The answer seemed to have satisfied the man as no further questions were asked on the subject. Zane was relieved as the timer went off and signaled the end of the event. Gliss reached down and looped her fingers through his as they walked down the hallway with the dean and Zack walking ahead of them. Zack was trying to get his uncle to tell him just how awesome he was. Gliss slowed them down, so they were out of earshot of the others, then she leaned in close, her lips brushed his ear, sending a wave of goosebumps shooting down his back.

"You were wonderful. This next year is going to be amazing. Zane, I was going to wait to tell you this but right now is as good a time as any… I think I love you."

Zane's heart took on a quicker than normal pace as he heard the last words fall off her lips. Zane wanted so badly to tell her the same, but the moment was interrupted by the dean's deep gruff voice.

"Um… are you guys coming? I wouldn't want you trapped in the hallway." Gliss pulled away from Zane and in her usual upbeat voice yelled, "we are coming!"

Daylight once again took hold of the earth as they exited the building. Zack tried to get them to come celebrate with him and the dean, but Gliss told them that they already had plans. They were left standing alone on the grassy hill just outside the General Studies Building.

"So… about what you said earlier," Zane was cut off by Gliss, who put her fingers to her lips, "Zane, you don't have to say it back, I know."

"Gliss… I want to, I have for a while now. Glissandra, I love everything about you. I am so grateful to have such a wonderful friend and, well, I guess, girlfriend now. I don't want to spend a minute without you by my side." Zane finished, his cheeks were red-hot, and he stared at the ground. Gliss pushed his head up so their eyes met.

"You can be my sidekick anytime." She said with a wink. Zane smiled and they decided another visit to Jan's Cafe was the best way to spend their evening. This time Zane convinced Jan to let him pay for the meal. Zane dropped Gliss off at her house, gave her a goodnight kiss and decided to fly to his parents' new place in the city. The flight would take him just over an hour and it was the perfect amount of time to let him process the day's events. Zane turned on some relaxing music and set a moderate speed. He let his mind drift.

Chapter 9

Shadows in the Dark

Zane was about twenty minutes into his flight when he noticed the dark figure flying close behind him. Zane reached up and twisted the dial on his helmet. He checked his flight channels. The lines were as quiet as a snowfall. Zane turned his communicator on and broadcasted on the shared frequency for all low flyers, "This is flier one eight two dash three. Please respond, unknown flier." The lines stayed silent, and Zane tried again.

"This is flier one eight two dash three, requesting identification of the flier in sector three-two delta. Altitude reading of three thousand and seven feet, bearing due south."

The mysterious flier behind Zane began to pick up speed; he aimed his body right towards Zane's. Zane kept the line open hoping for a response.

When it didn't come, he began to increase his speed. Zane had been practicing all summer on increasing his speed ever since that embarrassing incident with Zack. Zane had pushed himself and now he could nearly reach sixty miles an hour. Still the speed was considered slow; the mystery flier was hot on Zane's heels. Zane swerved to the east, changing his bearing. The flier did not attempt to hide his intent, as he followed Zane without skipping a heartbeat. Zane cursed under his breath and began to climb upwards. It was risky but Zane had been working hard on keeping a consistent speed even when climbing.

Zane watched as his altimeter rose. When Zane had climbed a good thousand feet, a hand grasped around his ankle. Zane kicked with his free leg and managed to break the assailant's grip on him. When he was free, Zane dove towards the ground. He welcomed the speed as he dove towards the dark landscape below. Zane was careful to keep the G-force to a bearable level. His radar indicated that his pursuer was gaining on him. Zane performed some evasive maneuvers he had learned while reading up on the superheroes of old. The figure followed his every move with ease.

Zane knew that the chase would soon be over, and he would be apprehended. In a desperate attempt to evade the attacker, Zane continued his dive down into the suburbs. He pulled up and scraped an elbow on the asphalt. The suit took the damage, and his elbow was left unscathed. Zane weaved in between two houses and through another backyard. His radar was picking up too much interference to be able to see if he was still being followed. Zane didn't slow down as he streaked down the darkened streets. He turned around, searching for the attacker. He slowed when he didn't see anyone behind him. Zane came to a stop and landed. He immediately regretted it, as a figure hit him in the back from behind. The two of them rolled in the street and Zane tried to take off from his position but a grasping hand restricted the take-off. Zane kicked and swung with his hands and feet, but they didn't make contact with his assailant.

A firm hand found its way under his helmet and began to squeeze around his throat. Zane struggled and rammed his head back smashing it into the attacker's helmet, there was a loud crack, and the hand released its grip. Zane immediately turned the knob on his helmet, emergency lights turned on in his suit casting a red hue into the darkened streets. Zane ran as fast as his feet could carry him. He glanced back and the man who had attacked him was in pursuit. Zane yelled into his intercom, "This is flier one eight two dash three! I am under attack by an unknown flier! He has forced me to the ground and is in pursuit with harmful intent. I am requesting assistance."

Static came across the line... Zane waited and continued to run, the dark-dressed man leapt into the air and began to take flight. Zane tripped himself and began to fly as well.

"Flyer one eight two dash three, police have been dispatched to your location, please wait for them to arrive." Zane didn't think he could just stop and wait for help to arrive, so he continued to evade.

"I can't wait as he is on my heels. Please help!" Zane yelled into the intercom, but no further response came.

"The police are on their way!" Zane yelled to the man behind him. The pursuer slowed slightly but then continued forward without a verbal response.

"Who are you?" Zane yelled, "and what do you want from me?"

The man caught up to him once more, but this time Zane was ready for his attack. The man lashed out with an arm and Zane barrel-rolled and grabbed the man's arm as he moved over the top of him. Zane pulled with all his might and threw the pair of them into a crazy spiral. Zane let go and the man spun away from him and crashed into the street below. Zane tried to pull out of the spiral, but he found himself skidding down the street. Pain registered in his head as he collided with a parked car. Alarms began to sound around him, but Zane found it nearly impossible to think, let alone get up. A gruff voice sounded next to his head.

"You win this time but the next time we meet I expect a better fight. See ya, Mr Whitlock." The voice disappeared and Zane lost consciousness. What happened over the next couple of hours was a blur to Zane. He could remember glimpses of people's faces, blaring lights, then his pain vanished and was replaced by bliss. Zane woke in a hospital room. He looked around at the monitors that beeped rhythmically. Then he noticed Gliss; she was curled up on a small couch with a blanket wrapped firmly around her. Zane smiled as he saw her shift slightly. *Where were his parents?* He thought to himself, all the memories of the night's events came flooding back to him. A shiver shot down his spine as he vividly reheard the words that were echoing around his head. The man who had attacked him had known his name, that was usually a bad thing, at least it was in movies and books.

Zane grabbed the remote that allowed him to control the hospital bed and he pressed the button that shifted him into a sitting position. The motors kicked on and hummed as the pneumatic piston raised him up. The subtle sound was enough to wake the slumbering Gliss, who was by his side in an instant.

"Oh, Zane, you're up. I've been so worried about you! Even though the doctors said you were going to be fine, I was still scared you would never wake up. When the hospital called, I rushed straight here. What happened?" Gliss said in a torrent of words. Zane tried to focus on the sentences, but he was having a difficult time keeping the words in the right order.

"Gliss, I…" Zane was having a hard time forming sentences of his own, but he pressed through the mental blockage.

"I'm okay. Why did the hospital call you, not parents?" The question came out not in the way he had intended but he was sure that Gliss deciphered it.

She looked at him, then placed a warm hand on his cheek, she leaned in and kissed him. "I'm just glad you're alright, I can tell you are having a hard time speaking, so I will do the talking. When your parents moved, I might have changed your emergency contact information so that I was the primary contact. Don't worry, I called your parents, and they are on their way over. You just get some rest before they get here." She kissed him once more then snuggled in on the bed with him. Zane didn't mind the company. His eyes began to droop once more. The effort of being awake this long had taken its toll and Zane nodded off to sleep.

The warm smell of cinnamon rolls drew him from his slumber and Zane's eyes flickered open. His parents stood in front of his bed. His mother was holding her phone out snapping pictures and his father was holding a plate with steaming cinnamon rolls that had warm gooey frosting slopped over the top of them. Zane's stomach growled and he realized just how hungry he was. Three more familiar faces shuffled into the room: Mr and Mrs Dunlap, with Travis taking up the rear. Zane smiled at everybody, which caused both mothers to give an audible, "aw".

Zane frowned. He had never gotten this reaction from smiling before and he began to wonder if it was the medication making him hallucinate. Understanding dawned as he felt Gliss squeeze his hand. Zane looked down and found her snuggled into his chest on the bed.

His cheeks burned with embarrassment which goaded a bout of laughter that filled the small, crowded hospital room. Gliss stirred then opened her eyes, she stretched and yawned then looked around the room. She waved and smiled at everyone, then her body went rigid. She noted the phones and cameras, all of which were aimed at her and Zane. She stood up and stepped away from Zane. The movement only caused more laughter and pictures to be taken.

"Put the phones, cameras, and other devices down now or else you will be searching for them at the bottom of the dumpster out back," Gliss growled, the audience immediately began to stash their devices away and order was restored to the room. Cinnamon rolls were soon distributed and all faces, and fingers were covered in the sugary, sticky, substance. Zane's stomach was satisfied, and he waited a couple of minutes as he listened to conversations that were budding around the room. Zane was finally able to understand the words, his head still hurt but he was relieved that he was able to think.

All the talking came to a stop when Gliss asked Zane what had happened to him. This time Zane recalled the night's events with clarity, and he told his story and even added in some extra roles and dives that had not happened. He left out the part about the man talking to him, he thought it would be best to only tell the police and maybe Gliss. His mother's hand was over her mouth and the men told each other their theories about why Zane had been targeted. Both men agreed that it was most likely a gang-related attack. A knock came at the door and a doctor stepped in.

"Would everyone except..." the doctor said, reading the name off the clipboard, "Glissandra Whitlock exit the room?"

Zane's parents looked at each other with shock, as did the Dunlaps. Questions and protests began to form at the backs of throats, but they were all ushered from the room before anyone could voice them. Travis ran up and gave Zane a fist bump before exiting the room. Zane was a little more than confused as he looked at Gliss who stared back at him with the same registered shock. The door closed hard behind them, and the doctor gestured for Gliss to take a seat. He looked at the clipboard once again.

"Whoopsy, Glissandra Dunlap, my darn dyslexia getting names flipped again." He looked up at the two of them, then back to the clipboard and continued. Zane relaxed as he recognized the honest mistake. For a second he had panicked that Gliss had done more than change his emergency contact information.

"Mr Whitlock, it is my job to tell you what procedures have been performed while you were unconscious and to tell you the condition you are in. When you were brought in to us, you suffered minor fractures to your right humerus, your left ulna, you had three broken ribs, a punctured lung and your spine had been compressed, resulting in temporary paralysis. You also suffered a minor concussion." He paused and took a breath before continuing. "We had to drain and patch your lung, set your ribs and, in order to restore the movement to your arms and legs, we had to place you in the anti-gravity chamber to allow your spine to decompress naturally. After our tests, it is concluded that you will make a full recovery and be able to return home within the next couple of days. If there is anything you need, feel free to call a nurse." He smiled then departed from the room. Zane couldn't believe all the damage he had sustained from the fight.

He had only been hit by a moving projectile at roughly sixty miles an hour, then spiraled out of control and smashed into a parked car. He didn't feel like it was enough to do all that damage, but, as he shifted in the bed he felt the pain in his chest, arms, legs, and back.

Gliss let out a slow whistle as she watched the doctor exit the room,

"Wow, they told me it was bad... but I didn't understand that much happened to you. Do you have a scar? I want to see." She said pulling down the front of his gown, Zane let her because he was just as curious about it. It was uglier than he had expected it to be; the flesh was bloody, and the stitches pulled the skin together in a gross-looking way.

"Wow, I wish I hadn't seen that," Gliss said, pulling the gown back up. Her face paled and she decided to go for a walk to get some fresh air. Zane was left in the room listening to his heartbeat on the monitor. He waited for a long while and a nurse popped in carrying a glass of water. She smiled at him and wrapped his chest with a fresh bandage. Zane asked her if he could go for a walk, and she said that would be a great idea. She helped him stand and even showed him how to support himself on the IV pole. Zane had made it to the front of the bed when Gliss made it back from her walk. The nurse was happy and asked Gliss if she wanted to help Zane go for a walk.

"Of course I do," she responded, then looped her arm through his. The walk was harder than Zane thought it would be. He made it down to the end of the hallway before he had to stop and catch his breath.

"Zane, are you doing all right?" Gliss asked.

Zane put on the bravest face he could muster and lied through his teeth, "I'm doing great, I just wanted to stop and breathe for a minute."

He smiled at her, trying to look as healthy as possible.

"Good, I'm glad."

"Hey, where did our parents go?" Zane asked, remembering that they were supposed to be outside the room.

"Oh… about that. Yeah, well… I ran into them briefly as they were being escorted out of the hospital. They aren't sure how it happened but, apparently, your dad said he was going to get a soda then walked off towards the vending machines. The next thing they knew he was strapped to a gurney and being wheeled down a different hallway shouting for help. Apparently, he was mistaken for an emotionally and mentally unstable patient who recently escaped their room. Everything got sorted out, but they were all asked to leave the hospital."

"That sounds like my dad," Zane said, smiling and grimacing simultaneously trying not to laugh. Gliss started laughing but quickly grew serious as she noticed how he winced when he chuckled.

She squeezed his hand and locked eyes with him. "Zane, can you promise me something?" she asked, her emerald, green eyes glittering from the LED lights above.

"Yeah, anything," he replied.

"Don't ever fly without me. Okay? If I was there, we could have kicked his butt," she said, eyes burning with fire. Zane smiled and promised her he wouldn't fly without her again. They headed back to the hospital room. When they got there Zane froze because the dean stood with arms clasped behind his back. Gliss finally nudged him, and Zane allowed her to help him back into the bed. The dean turned around after Zane was settled. Gliss and Zane both gasped and they saw the black eye, cuts, and bruises that ran up and down his body.

"Dean Richardson, what happened to you?" Gliss asked.

"I'm glad you're both okay. I was afraid something might have happened to both of you. I can see that they only reached Zane. For that I am sorry." The dean moved over to the door and closed it, then he walked over to the window and pulled the curtains closed.

"Last night Zack and I were attacked. It seemed to be an organized attempt to silence us. As you are aware, there are some on the council who despise the idea of a hero course and, as much as it pains me to say this, the individuals that voted against you are both from powerful families. I would hate to point an accusing finger, but the men that attacked last night were extremely skilled and seemed to know a great deal about both mine and Zack's powers."

"Is Zack okay?" Zane asked the dean.

"Zack will be fine. He escaped with little more than a broken finger. I thought that I had been the only target, but when I heard about Zack, I began to feel more and more like this was a coordinated attack to stop us at any cost. Zane, I need to know every detail about what happened to you last night," the dean demanded. Zane felt like he had been punched in the gut after hearing the story from the dean. Zane told the story but this time he left out the added rolls and dives. Instead he gave the real ending to the story including the man who had called him by name. Zane watched as the dean's face fell into a deep grimace.

"As soon as you are well, please come see me at my house. I will do everything I can in the meantime to protect both of you. When you are discharged, don't fly, don't take a cab; I will send Zack over to pick you up and take you home. If what I suspect is true, then this is just the beginning." With that, the dean walked out of the room leaving the two of them alone listening to the sounds of beeping machinery.

"Gliss, do you think that we are going to be safe?"

Gliss, usually full of so much fire and optimism said, "I don't know, Zane, I wish I could tell you yes."

The night was long and sleepless, even with Gliss curled up to one side of him. Zane couldn't sleep. Every time he closed his eyes, he saw the impending doom that awaited them outside the hospital. The next morning his doctor gave him the discharge papers and, the next thing Zane knew, they were being shuttled to the dean's house by Zack, who try as he might to cheer them up, failed miserably. Zane was as gray as a heavy rain cloud, one that could not simply be blown away by the surrounding winds. He would not, could not, be cheered up by anyone. Today was simply a miserable day to live through.

Chapter 10

Heroes Training

Gliss sat next to the lump that was her boyfriend. Zane had chosen to be a bland, gray, dismal person today. It didn't bother Gliss much, but she sure missed his smile. She sighed as they bounced around in the back seat of the large vehicle. The chair in front of her was absolutely humongous; it stretched across the front of the car covering three quarters of the distance to the passenger's side door. The chair on the passenger side was ridiculously small. Gliss didn't even think a toddler would fit in the seat. The interior of the car was roomy, and the seats were extremely comfortable. The only thing that scared her about the car was its driver. Gliss had never seen so many obscene gestures from other drivers in a single car ride.

Zack drove the way he talked; slow and easy going. He allowed himself to meander into the other lanes on the road resulting in frightened drivers swerving out of his way. He didn't use his blinkers, claiming it was the best way to ensure they would work when he really needed to use them.

More than once, Gliss's fingernails pierced Zane's skin. Yet even the pain of her fingers digging into his flesh did not get a reaction bigger than, "Gliss... Gliss you can let go now," from Zane. His mood was affecting her. She was relieved as they pulled into the driveway. Gliss helped Zane from the car, and they followed Zack into the house. They entered the concrete structure and Zack led them to a set of stairs that spiraled down into a darkened space below. The metal stairs rang out as a calling card to all who hid below. They circled down further and further until small lights set into the concrete began to shine a dull, blue light illuminating the stairs in front of them. They walked down further into the depths of the impossibly deep room. Zack clapped his hands twice in the air and lights above them began to flicker on. Gliss couldn't comprehend what she saw: large marble pillars shot up towards a shiny black ceiling above, display cases lined the walls; their contents sparked her interest. Zane's rain cloud dispersed instantly. Zane literally glided from display case to display case.

"Gliss, do you know what this stuff is?" he asked excitedly.

"Not really," she said, looking at a pair of shiny gloves that were gold and blue, with sharp points jutting out from the knuckles. Zack had disappeared.

"These are first edition gloves, they even look used, which doesn't make them just rare, but extremely valuable. These gloves are from one of the last real superheroes in history. Merely Justice. He retired just over twenty years ago. He was a sidekick for some real powerful *superheroes,* not just the heroes we are used to. I'll admit, not the catchiest name, but the name doesn't matter when the superhero does incredible things."

Zane floated off to another display case set into the wall. Gliss watched as excited shrieks and babbling came from Zane; she had never seen him geek out so much in his entire life.

A sound like crashing boulders exploded from down a corridor. Gliss instinctively stepped away from the noise as the dean burst through the entrance, sweat forming on his forehead.

Seeing him, Zane suddenly shouted, "No way! Dean Richardson you were Merely Justice?"

Gliss noted the flashy blue and gold outfit the dean was wearing. His muscles bulged in the suit.

"That was a long time ago, besides the name was stupid. I haven't gone by that name for over twenty years. I haven't done any hero work in twenty years either," he said, rubbing his chin as if he were lost in thought, reliving the glory days in his mind.

"I can't believe you were Merely Justice this whole time and no one even knew it!" Zane squealed, edging closer and circling the dean making mental notes of every part of his costume, as he simultaneously battered him with questions.

"Who was your favorite hero to work with? Why did you retire? Why did you choose to be a sidekick?

With a power like yours it should have been easy to be a first-rate hero. Did you come up with your own name? Did you ever think about changing it?"

Instead of waiting for answers, the questions continued to pour out of Zane like water spurting from a newly drilled-well. Gliss watched as Zane stared with sparkling childlike wonder at a true hero. For the first time, Gliss understood how much Zane admired heroes. She would have to ask him more about it later when they were alone. After all, it wasn't like heroes were in the news or anything any more; no one really talked about them except for in their history classes. It seemed like nowadays the media treat powers like extra special disabilities.

"Now, this kind of thing is exactly why I never told anyone I was Merely Justice. What matters right now is that we need to get you three in shape to teach some future heroes and that means I have a lot of teaching to do."

The dean puffed up his chest as he spoke, and Zane began to look like he might faint and start drooling. Gliss leaned over and assisted Zane in closing his gaping mouth.

"What's first?" Gliss said, getting rather excited herself. Zane must be rubbing off on me, she thought.

The dean started them off with some basic strength and endurance training which wasn't horribly hard but wasn't a major part of their day-to-day life up until now. After all they were not athletes. They were in the general studies course. Of course, Zane was too injured to participate, so he basically bounced around annoying everyone while Gliss and Zack were sweating profusely engaged in one physical activity or another, with the dean constantly giving pointers, critique, or fun facts about said exercises.

After the first day, Zane began to realize the dean wasn't going to give up any trivia answers and that his endless questions only made him mad, resulting in more relentless cardio for the other two. This led to Zane attempting to cheerlead and/or create extremely stupid modifications to the exercises, to the point that a ninety-year-old man in a wheelchair would have no trouble joining in and also manage not to feel winded. After about a week of this, the dean began to "teach" them some basic self-defense. He pulled up videos on the internet with a really buff dude teaching some young pretty girl to escape.

"Honestly, I feel like we should be insulted," Zane said as the video continued. "This is bad enough without your commentary," Gliss said, shooting him a glare.

"Yeah, man, how come I have to be the defenseless girl?" Zach said from his position under Gliss.

She shot him a glare that was much more menacing than the one Zane had received. Gliss was fuming. It wasn't enough that she had spent every night this week sleeping like a brick and also too tired to get up in the morning, but now they were being insulted. The dean could at least teach them some real fighting moves. And where had he gone? He disappeared while they were reenacting videos and hadn't reappeared.

"Tap out, tap out!" Zack yelled.

Gliss realized that she was nearly breaking his arm and quickly released him.

"Sorry I got distracted," she apologized.

"Man, and here I was thinking you being distracted might make you go easy on me," Zack said while tenderly cradling his arm and stepping back several steps.

"Why don't you beat up your boyfriend for a minute while I recuperate?" he said while walking over to a side table where a small teapot sat. He poured himself a cup of mildly warm tea and sat down cross-legged on a pillow. Still sipping his tea.

Gliss rolled her eyes and looked over to Zane who was trying to communicate with his eyes that he was still too injured to be brutally tortured. She walked over and sat down next to him while letting out a huge sigh.

"Where do you think he even went?"

"Into his own world, I suppose," Zane replied while looking over his shoulder at Zack, now hovering inches above the pillow with a gentle humming sound.

"What?" Gliss said, looking over at him and following his gaze.

"I meant the dean," she said, rolling her eyes.

"Oh , now that you mention it, he has been gone for quite a while hasn't he."

"Did he say he was going somewhere?" Gliss asked.

"No, but I'm sure he is doing something important," Zane replied with an awe-like wonder as he imagined what villains he must be fighting on his way around the school.

"I think you are a little too trusting," Gliss said, a small grin forming. This was the most they had really gotten a chance to talk. It wasn't that the dean was like a drill sergeant, rather he seemed like an exercising enthusiast. They found they were normally too out of breath to converse, aside from Zane making stupid comments and Gliss rolling her eyes, of course.

"Speaking of disappearances, where did Zack go?" Zane said while motioning to the now-empty corner with a matching empty teacup.

"No way, where did he go? I never even heard him get up."

Suddenly Zach burst in the main door wearing what looked like an oversized sweater with a hood and mask, all of which appeared to be both knitted and tie-dyed. He was also wearing a bright red pair of cargo pants and dinosaur spikes running up the back of the sweater that appeared to be made of the same fabric as the pants.

"Hey guys, check it out."

Both Gliss and Zane sat in silence taking in the costume.

"A buddy of mine raises alpacas and I have been experimenting with homemade dyes." he said, turning around so that Gliss and Zane could see his horrific costume from every angle.

"And, well, the pants I just ordered online. Pretty cool, huh?" he said, while striking a dramatic pose.

"How did you even have time to make this?" Gliss said, thinking about how soundly she had slept the last week.

"Well, I don't really sleep much so just here a little and there a little. Also, one of my vintage buddies offered to help make the mask when I asked him for some pointers."

Just in time, the dean walked through the door and immediately spewed hot tea everywhere and began to cough attempting to suck in air. When he finally caught his breath, he shouted,

"Zack, where in the world did you get that thing!" He cut Zack off before he could answer and said,

"Never mind, it's obviously homemade. Zane, since you have nothing better to do, do you think you could help him come up with something that isn't going to fill up with sweat like a sponge."

Zane began to protest but the dean continued, "The computer lab down the hall should have adequate programs for drawing up some plans. Take scans of both Gliss and Zack so you can get the dimension information you need. When you come up with something satisfactory, I will let you print up a prototype on the school's 3D printers."

Gliss watched as Zane headed off down the hall. He came back a moment later with a scanner. He scanned both her and Zack before heading off back in the direction of the computer lab. The rest of the day was tedious and unforgiving. Gliss could feel nearly every muscle in her body aching when she caught a ride home from her mother. Gliss was curious what Zane would come up with for her suit; the thought began to excite her. Sleep didn't come easy as, every time she tossed in her bed, pain coursed through her body. Eventually, she found a way to sleep and nodded off.

Chapter 11

Suits, Students, Success

Zane spent the next two weeks in the computer lab, not just designing suits for Zack and Gliss, but for himself and the dean as well. The work was surprisingly fun for Zane, and he found himself remembering the little material he had learned from the shared classes with Gliss. He remembered the different types of fabrics that one could use for different purposes. Of course, Zane had to pass off his ideas to Gliss and the Dean before he was allowed to print the suits.

Zane had gone with a simple yet elegant suit for Gliss, gaining inspiration from her hot pink flight suit. Zane worked night and day to design her suit so it could be powered by her glitter spheres. He felt a hint of pride at his work as he looked over the final renderings. Zane printed them off and downloaded a copy of all his work to the main computer system.

Zane walked down the hallway and back to the training ground. He was feeling much stronger now that his scar and his lung had healed. The doctor had cleared him for any physical activity and given him a lollipop, sending him on his way with a note written to the dean. Zane was actually excited to work out and learn from the dean. He turned the corner and entered the training space where the dean was hanging from a bar and doing pull-ups. The metal bar had to be over three inches thick. Zane fell forward and floated up to the dean whose face was burning red with exertion.

"Hey, dean, I finished up on the designs and I'm ready to print them."

He looked at Zane and cocked an eyebrow. "You're done already? Back when I designed and made my suit it took months. Good job on finishing up Zack's suit."

Zane laughed weakly. "Yeah, not just Zack's suite, but Gliss's too and one or two designs for your new suit, and one for me," Zane said with a smile. The dean dropped to the ground with a thud. The floor shook beneath him.

"Well, let's see them," the dean said, grabbing a towel from a nearby rack. "Zack, Gliss. Zane has something to show us."

Zack turned his head to look at the dean, but Gliss had already started a punch and, by the time Zack noticed it, was too late; her fist connected with his face. There was a yelp of pain and Zack fell to the ground. Gliss did not show any concern, instead she just skipped over to them, leaving Zack on the ground. The dean chuckled; it was an eerie sound to hear coming from the man.

"Hey, guys, what's up?" Gliss said with a smile. Zack finally pulled himself to his feet and walked over, joining the group.

"Let's go to the computer lab and use the 3D projection chamber." the dean said, a smile still on his face as he led the way down the hallway and to the computer lab. Zane uploaded the files to the projection chamber and the four of them put on the goggles that would allow them to interact with the projections. Minutes later, the suits began to take form and Zane walked up inspecting each suit. He grabbed them and handed the digitals out to the group. Gliss squealed as she saw her suit, unable to contain her excitement. Zane walked over to her and began to show her the ins and outs of her suit. He accessed the source code and pulled specific pieces out to show her the intricate system of tubes. Zane pulled up her shoes and separated the pieces to show her what he had done.

"So, we know that your spheres already gather in your shoes, ingeniously I have added a chamber here and, with the press of a button on your arm control panel, you can break individual spheres. The chamber is rated for thirty thousand pounds per square inch. You can break up to three spheres in each shoe. The pressure can be routed through your suit for different things." Zane stepped back and pulled on the back of her suit and two places on her sleeves. "You can use the built-up pressure to make you fly; the two on the arm sleeves allow you to steer. The chamber's pressure also fuels two other places on your suit," he pointed to small holes hidden in the arms. "You can load spheres that will be stored in different places around the suit. You can shoot your spheres like weapons. Again, you can control the speed at which they will be fired. The suit automatically adjusts your shot pressure based on your target. It is designed to be strong enough to break the glass but not skin, since that could be… bad," Zane said as the rest of them winced at the thought.

"There is one last feature that I have added just in case of a fall. If you fall, your suit will analyze how dangerous the impact will be. If the situation warrants it, your suit will deploy an airbag system." Zane stepped back and put all the pieces back together, letting Gliss see the suit in full once more.

"Wow! Zane, how long did you spend on this?" Gliss asked him.

"It didn't take me that long…" Zane said before walking over to Zack.

Zane watched as his roommate was trying to figure out how to tell the program to put it on his body. Zane approached him. He had based the new design off the original alpaca version. He thought he had improved upon the design. The spikes were made of carbon fiber and the helmet had a reptilian look, complete with teeth. The gloves had retractable claws. When Zack wanted to, he could use the control panel on his arm to make the claws extend.

"Zack, you can't put it on until it's been printed, as long as you don't gain any weight, the suit will fit." Zane went on to show his friend all the different features built into the suit. Zack nearly cried when he saw the retractable claws. Zane finally stepped over to the dean whose suit was flashier than his old one. To prove a point, Zane had woven in 'Merely Justice' into the front of the suit. The large man stood in silence for a long time.

"It will never work. It looks really well-designed, but I will end up breaking the suit in a matter of minutes if I were to wear this," the dean said, ashamed.

"I don't know what you are talking about. I have made all the adjustments to your suit, which was the hardest, because I know that, as you change, your density the pressure you exude on the clothing is extreme and it has to hold up, especially when you punch, kick or jump. I took a sample of your old suit, and I took the liberty of working with Gliss on a new, even stronger material. It will match the density of your body up to that of tungsten. The fabric is new, but Gliss is convinced we can make it." The Dean stepped back in awe.

"How do you know what my power is?" Zane shrunk back slightly before answering.

"Well, at first, it was just a guess, after watching every fight you were ever part of. I questioned Zack and he filled me in on the rest. Please don't be mad at him. I told him you told me to ask him about it," Zane said, stepping further away from him. The heated response did not come, instead the dean clapped Zane on the shoulder and said, "thank you."

Zane walked over to his suit. It was sleek and black. The helmet was shaped like a teardrop. Zane had equipped small fins that could move up and down on his sides, feet, and arms. He had one central fin that rose out of the back of his suit. They would provide him with the edge he needed to make near impossible maneuvers in the sky. Zane had secretly hidden small jet engines on either shoulder. He had pulled a design from an archive of an old theoretical engine that would be self-sustaining as he flew. The device would pull the different gases from the atmosphere and turn them into raw fuel, as long as he was able to contribute to it with some of his own propulsionary power. Zane had already ordered all the pieces for the device, along with the two engines. It had taken all his funds to purchase the equipment.

Zane had been staring at his suit so intently that he hadn't realized that the others had joined him around the suit. Zane stepped back and let everyone examine it. There were a few oohs and aws from his friends. Then the dean stepped away and clapped his hands together.

"Well done, Zane, now you only have to design and help make seven more for your students."

Zane went rigid. *Students, there were going to be seven students? How long had the dean known this information?*

"We are getting students?" Gliss asked excitedly.

"Yes, the list came in this morning. I will forward the email with all their contact information on it. Now the real work starts. Zane, I want you to stay late here to begin your training." the dean said.

The training was more intense than Zane had imagined. Gliss had offered to stay and be his sparring partner. Zane wished Zack had stayed as he rubbed his arms that had taken a beating from Gliss. Zane repeated a series of movements designed to defend himself from an attacker with a knife. The dean yelled at them from across the room.

"Let's call it a day, you will need your rest so we can get you caught up on the time you lost recovering the last two weeks." They said their goodbyes and Zane, for the first time in two weeks, flew Gliss home. He probably shouldn't have, considering the condition his suit was in; tears on the elbows, knees, and the giant crack in his helmet. The communications knob was broken so the flight was quiet and Gliss tried to use hand signals to talk with him. That did not work, so she just gave up until they arrived. Zane unclipped Gliss and they walked in through the front door.

"Oh hello, Mrs Whitlock. It's nice to see you have brought your husband home with yo,." Gliss's father said. The comment brought a quick smack from Mrs Dunlap. Travis was the first to give into the laughter. Zane had completely forgotten about the embarrassing moment at the hospital.

Gliss turned bright red but didn't move to correct them, Zane smiled and waved. Once the laughter had subsided, Mrs Dunlap gestured for the two of them to take a seat at the table. Zane made his way over and sat down. Soon a large glass of milk was set in front of him along with a sleeve of chocolate cream-filled cookies. Zane and Gliss took turns dunking the popular cookies in the milk then quickly consuming them before they turned to mush between fingers on the way to their mouths. Soon the sleeve was empty and normal conversation sparked.

Gliss told her parents about the suits that Zane had designed for them. The comment brought a look of worry on Gliss's mom's face. It was gone in a flash, but Zane was sure that he had noticed. Questions about his scar came up and Zane said that he was fully recovered. No one else brought up the night of the attack and Zane soon dismissed himself from the group. He gave Gliss a quick kiss and told her that he would call her later. Zane fell off the front steps and he flew as quickly as his body would let him home. No attackers showed up during his flight. Zane was relieved that things were going back to normal. He walked into his apartment that had somehow accumulated more piles of junk. Zane set to work cleaning. He did all his laundry and some of Zack's laundry that had found its way into Zane's stuff. Once Zane finished with the dishes, he took a quick shower and pulled on some clean clothes. As he was about to sit down and turn on the TV, there was a knock at the door.

Zane stood up and walked over, peered through the spy hole to find a delivery man standing with three boxes. Zane undid the locks and the short man in the short shorts handed him a clipboard.

"Sign on the dotted line. I do have to say that you got some pretty cool stuff, what are you like a scientist?" Zane finished signing the paper and absentmindedly told the man.

"No, I'm a high school teacher."

"Nice, well enjoy," the man said, taking the clipboard back from Zane. He was left trying to move the boxes into his apartment. They were so heavy. When he finally got them into the apartment, Zane was sweating. He quickly opened the first box and found all the carbon fiber and different metal alloys he had ordered. Zane pushed it aside and opened the next one. Two gleaming jet engines sat inside, along with a variety of different metal parts, wires and an instruction manual. Zane beamed at the engines. He pulled one out and examined it closely, then closed the box and pushed it down the hall into his room. Then he came back and opened the last box. Fabric exploded from the interior and spilled out onto the carpet. Zane rummaged through the different materials and examined them. When Zack got home, Zane asked for his help taking the boxes to the school;, all except the last one which he left at home. They arrived and took the boxes down to their new classroom. Zane found Gliss inside hanging decorations on the walls with her headphones on, bobbing her head to match the beat of the music.

"Gliss" Zane yelled as they pushed the boxes through the opening. She nearly fell off the ladder she was balancing on.

"Oh, hey, you guys. You got my text about decorating the room?" she asked them.

Zane shot a look at Zack, saying, "don't say anything."

"Yeah, we also got our order, so we can 3D print our suits and start assembling them," Zane replied.

The promise to start working on Zack's suit was enough to buy his silence about not reading the group text.

"Really?" Gliss asked excitedly, as she rushed over to the boxes and flung the lids open. She began rummaging through the materials. She separated them out and organized them by color, make, and strength.

"Let's forget about decorating the classroom today. Let's help Zane with anything he needs."

Together they moved the boxes down the hallway and to the 3D printing lab. They arrived and Zane flipped on the lights to the familiar room. He took a deep breath then set to work warming up the different machines. He separated out the different alloys, metals, and carbon fibers. Then he showed Gliss where to arrange the different fabric. Once all the machines were prepped and all the materials laid out, Zane plugged in the first suit's designs; Gliss's. He hit the print button and the machines began to hum.

"So, how long does it take?" Gliss asked, looking at Zane.

"I don't know, let me check what it says."

Zane's hands flew over the keyboard as he accessed the timeline.

"It says, two hours and thirteen minutes," Zane said, looking at her.

She frowned, "I don't know if I can wait that long," Gliss said.

"That's just to print the husk. I still have hours of tweaking and electrical work ahead of me, before it is usable," Zane said which only made Gliss frown deeper.

"It's okay though, I can start printing the other three suits too. Help me with the other printers," Zane said standing up.

They followed him and they arranged materials, metals, and fabrics all over again. Once all the machines were humming, they walked back to their classroom. The decorating took longer than the suits did. Gliss was so particular about every poster and the position of all the different bows and dots that it took hours to complete. Zane walked back to the 3D printing lab. He picked up the suits, then shut down the machines and logged out. Zack's car was full of helmets, shoes, gloves, suits, claws, visors, and a variety of wires, tubes, buttons, switches, and interfaces.

Zane sighed as he looked at the task ahead. Zack offered to help Zane when they got home but he refused, saying that he would work on it later. Zane and Zack finally opened the email the dean had sent over to them containing the names and contacts of their new students.

Zane read aloud for the two of them, "Ruby Raviras, Henry Laundreaux, RoseAnne Abbott, Calvin Smith, Logan Gardner, Evelyn Burke, and Simon Spitzout". Some of the names sounded familiar to Zane; he was sure when he saw their faces that he would recognize them. Most of them were going to be juniors this year, there was only one senior.

It reminded Zane of the timeline they were on. If they had been given the proper amount of time they would have given the class two years at least to show success. Simon was going to be the only senior this year so he would have to be their main focus if they wanted the system to succeed. Seeing the names somehow made it all feel so real. Zane flipped open his phone and looked at the calendar. He groaned as he saw that school would start in less than six weeks. So much of the summer had already passed and the school year would soon be upon them. Zack walked away and kept trying to find different rhymes that would help him remember the names on the list. Zane retired to his bedroom to begin working on the suits. The work would help him focus and help him forget his worries so he would be able to sleep. Zane looked at the clock and read the numbers, eleven thirty-two.

The night was still young, so Zane began the assembly process. It was long and tedious work. It took just over three hours to wire and assemble Gliss's suit.

Deciding that the night was over, Zane began his early morning. He grabbed an energy drink from the refrigerator then headed back to his room. Zack's suit did not take as long; he finished it within an hour. He finished the dean's and set to work on his own. Zane's took the remainder of the morning, and it was well after nine thirty when Zack knocked and opened his door. He froze as he looked at Zane, who sat in a hard chair wearing a pair of glasses and a loupe held in front of one eye, soldering the last piece of his jetpack system. Zane looked up at Zack.

"Good morning, Zack, how did you sleep?"

"Good. I'm not even going to ask if you slept because it is kind of obvious that you did not. How many energy drinks did you have last night?"

Zane looked around the room. He noticed four empty cans on the ground.

"I had a few, but look what I did," Zane held out Zack's suit to him, helmet and all. Zack greedily accepted the suit then raced out the door. Zane relaxed slightly then slid the device into its slot on the back of his suit. He connected the last wires and closed the compartment. Zane didn't feel like waiting either and began to pull on the suit.

Once it was on, he activated the interface. The computer loaded for a moment then diagnostics began to run, he waited, then the screen flashed green three times and the display came online. The diagnostic results were read to him by the computer. Zane tried the different fins and he felt them move on his body. Zack came back into the room he held his arm out for Zane to examine.

"Man, I think it's broken. It keeps saying that my claws are locked!"

"It's not broken. The safety is on. I thought a slow tryout would be better," Zane said.

"Come on, Zane, I want to see the claws work."

Zane entered the pin he had set so that Zack wouldn't be able to access his whole suit's potential and he explained how to use the claws. He stepped back and watched as the claws shot out and then retracted. Zane showed Zack the ones he hid in the shoes to make it easier to climb with, if he needed, and to make his kicks more effective. Zack tried the claws in his feet, and Zane could hear the shouts of joy coming from the inside of Zack's helmet.

"So, you want to go give your uncle his suit and I will go grab Gliss?"

"Yeah, bro, let's meet at my uncle's."

Zane and Zack raced towards the door, each of them had a backpack with a suit hidden inside. They burst out the apartment door. Zane hurriedly closed the door and followed Zack off the balcony. There was a shriek that came from below.

Zane looked at their downstairs neighbor Mrs Reynolds. She was pointing at Zack, whose claws and spikes had shot out as he jumped from the balcony towards her. He paused once he was hovering and removed his visor.

"Good morning, Mrs Reynolds, it's a wonderful day, right?"

"Is that you, Zack? You look like some kind of reptile."

"Yeah, it's my new superhero suit, do you like it?"

"Sure. But next time could you warn someone before you jump down at them?"

"Yeah, sure, well, we will talk to you later, Mrs Reynolds."

"Okay, 'bye, deary."

They waved and Zane took off upwards. He monitored the gas build-up in his jet pack; it was roughly twenty percent full. When Zane turned on the jet engines, he heard the classic whine as they began to turn and he primed them, then ignited the engines. For a minute, he was dismayed as they continued to spin without igniting. Zane sped up as they finally lit. He set them at a ten percent thrust. The acceleration was fantastic, and he watched as his speed increased to eighty miles an hour. Zane had to make a U-turn as he passed Gliss's house. He shut down the engines and slowed as he landed on Gliss's front porch. He kept his helmet on as he rang the doorbell. Travis answered the door.

"Woah, who are you?"

Zane pressed the button on the side of his helmet, the visor shot up.

"Zane, you look awesome!"

"Thanks, Travis, is Gliss around?"

"Yeah, she is downstairs. She has been getting her hair ready for twenty minutes," Travis said using air quotes as he emphasized the amount of time Gliss had been in the bathroom.

"Could you take this to her and tell her it is from me. She might be another twenty minutes; I will wait upstairs."

Zane handed the backpack to Travis, and he took off towards the stairs. Zane heard Travis fall down the stairs with a clattering backpack following behind him. Zane walked over to the stairwell and peered down at Travis who lay in a heap on the floor below.

"You all right?" Zane asked, looking down at the smaller boy. Zane noted the top zipper on the backpack was partially open. Zane assumed it was the reason for Travis's tumble down the stairs.

"Yeah," came the grumbled reply, as Travis peeled himself off the concrete floor below. He saw the younger boy cradling an arm as he slunk off towards the bathroom. Zane knew the backpack had arrived when shrieks of happiness and joy exploded from the basement below. He actually thought he heard her cry for a moment. Travis came back up from the basement. He was still clutching his injured arm.

"You owe me, I was thinking, for my troubles, maybe you could make me a suit?" Travis said, making sure that Zane saw his injured arm. Zane shook his head and with a grin responded.

"I will have to look into that." The sound of pounding feet coming up the stairs interrupted their conversation. Gliss emerged wearing her bright, new, shiny, suit. It had stripes of black running through it, giving the suit a more menacing look.

"Zane, how long did you stay up last night?" Gliss asked as her visor slid up revealing her face.

"I didn't sleep much, if that is what you mean," Zane responded, the exhaustion beginning to tug at his consciousness. Zane brushed it away as Gliss demanded a demonstration of how to operate the suit. Zane was glad he had installed the parental controls on both Zack and Gliss's suits. He hadn't put one on his or the dean's, figuring that he was competent to operate his suit freely. Zane had added in some spikes that could jut out of his knuckles; other than that the dean's suit was not as special as the others. Zane remembered that he had given access to Zack to operate all his controls and the worry set in. Gliss spun around in a circle so that the viewers could see the entirety of the suit in its perfection.

"I will show you everything about your suit, but your living room is not the right space. We should go somewhere no one will see us or be bothered by the glitter. I made a mistake and gave Zack full access to his suit, so we need to hurry before he accidentally impales the dean." Gliss gave him a pouty lip, but Zane pulled on Gliss's arm and together they stepped out into the world.

Zane strapped Gliss in then checked the fuel tank on the jet engines; the display read sixty percent. So, Zane walked out into the yard, standing a good distance away from any large obstructions. The engines lit and began to whine. Gliss came on over the communications tab.

"Zane, do you hear that noise? Is something wrong?" Gliss asked worriedly.

"No, I just added in a feature that allows us to take off from the ground." Zane set the thrust to fifteen percent. The suit had done the math for him adjusting for the additional weight strapped to his chest. The two of them launched off from the ground, the rush of speed took the breath out of Zane.

"Ah," he heard Gliss scream over the speakers. Zane would have screamed too but his brain was trying to force the command out of his mouth. Zane felt like his mouth was incapable of movement. They continued to soar higher and higher through the air gaining speed. The command finally shot out from his mouth, spittle forcing its way down the corners of his mouth and into his ears. The engines slowed and Zane leveled them out. The new fins corrected the errors in his flight path. Zane set the destination and for the first time as he joined the flyway, exhilaration coursed through his veins as he looked at the world below.

"Don't ever do that again," Gliss said.

"You're telling me that you didn't enjoy that?"

"Zane, if you do that again I will retract my statement about flying with only you," she threatened.

"Fine… Fine you win. Next time we will go twice as fast," Zane said jovially. The microphone went silent then music began to blast through Zane's helmet. The song was fast paced and had catchy lyrics. Zane knew that even if she turned it off now there would be no saving him from a day of quietly humming, or singing the song to himself.

"You're a monster, you know that, right?"

"What? Little old me? A monster? I just wanted to show you one of my favorite songs," Gliss said sarcastically. The song eventually ended and sure enough the song began to play on a loop in Zane's head. They landed at the dean's house and, without knocking, entered the front door code and walked in.

The dean stood in his new suit. Zack faced him and to Zane's horror, Zack was relentlessly delivering a series of blows at the dean with spikes at their full length. Zane felt the ground shudder beneath him with every blow. Zack noticed them for the first time and stepped back retracting the claws on his suit. The dean looked up then smiled at them.

"I don't know how you did it but, the suit doesn't rip, it holds up to everything," the dean said, stepping forward allowing Zane and Gliss to examine the suit. Other than small scratches on the suit, there was no other visible damage. The rest of the day was truly terrible as suits were put away and training began. Zane felt his arms burning as he did pushups. The dean switched up the program each day so they were working different muscle groups. He also showed them how to use every part of their body as a weapon.

He explained, "Most people think that punching is the best way to fight. If you thought this then you were wrong. The fists are weak and fragile; there are so many things that can go wrong with a punch that is thrown improperly." The dean demonstrated in slow motion just how many different ways a punch could go wrong before continuing.

"There are far more effective ways of defeating your opponents; you can use your elbows, knees, and shoulders." The dean went on to demonstrate a series of different movements that safely allowed you to attack with power and precision.

The rest of the summer went on in a similar fashion. The last two weeks were upon them in a flash and the dean gave them the week off to get the paperwork to the students. Gliss and Zane had been given five out of the seven students. The Dean and Zack had agreed to help the last two with the paperwork. Zane and Gliss landed gently on the front porch of a lavish looking house. The neighborhood was gated. Zane had never been to a neighborhood with a gate before. He unhooked Gliss and she stepped up beside him.

"I call ringing the doorbell!" Gliss said, racing forward and pressing the small button. A melodious song began to ring through the colorful house showering them with delightful tones. The door opened and an unfamiliar face stepped out to join them. Ruby Reviras stood taller than Gliss; she had long blonde hair, neatly separated into two ponytails. She had piercing blue eyes with long eyelashes, and wore a deep blue dress that hung around her ankles. Her fingernails were painted in a variety of colors, ranging from deep purples, to blinding pink, hints of green and orange popped out as well. Her skin was pale which only made her eyes all the more serious. She looked like some kind of princess out of a fairytale.

"Can I help you?" she asked, looking at Zane and Gliss who stood in their shining suits. Zane removed his helmet and Gliss followed suit.

"Yes, are you Ruby Reviaras?" Zane asked.

"Who's asking?" she snapped.

"Well, I'm Mr Whitlock, and this is Ms Dunlap. We were informed you have enrolled in the hero course. We are here to get you a head start on some of this year's paperwork; the faster we can get some of the forms signed and sent out, the better your experience will be in our course," Zane said, sounding as professional as he could.

"Oh, I thought you were some kind of weirdos asking for money or something. You guys can come right on in," she said, waving a hand over her shoulder ushering them into her home.

Zane had never been inside a bigger house. It was like a castle and Ruby was the princess that lived inside. Zane was waiting for a knight in shining armor to show up at the front door. They walked down a long corridor. The marble hallway was polished so well, Zane could see his reflection. Gliss glanced over towards him, and her eyes contained the same childlike wonder that he was experiencing.

The hallway broadened then opened into a large dining room, hand-hewn wooden chairs sat around a large table made from solid obsidian. The chandeliers that dangled from above glittered as light reflected through the crystal, casting a beautiful array of different colors on the walls and floors.

Ruby pulled one of the chairs out then asked, "Are you going to sit down or are we going to do this standing?"

Zane and Gliss both made their way over to the table and sat down.

"So, you have some papers for me to sign? Let's see them." Ruby held her hand out waiting for Zane to hand her the clipboard.

"Don't you want to know a little more about what to expect in our class? Or what to expect to be doing?"

"That's what the first day of school is for. Listen, I have a very busy schedule, can we hurry this up a bit?" Ruby asked, her patience wearing thin.

"Ruby, may I ask why you enrolled in the hero program?" Gliss asked.

"It was the most practical decision. There was no other option that caught my eye. I couldn't be a part of any other program. I don't do needles. I don't shoot guns and I don't like reading history books. I like to draw, paint and be awesome. So, when they gave me the option to switch, it was the easiest thing I have ever done."

"Oh well, good. Do you mind if you tell us a little more about your power so that way we can better prepare ourselves."

"I can change the colors of objects, watch." Ruby tapped her finger on the obsidian table-top and the entire surface turned a brilliant red. She let go and the tabletop returned to its normal black. Zane took out his notepad and began to scribble.

"So, what papers do I need to sign?" Ruby asked again. Zane looked up from his notes then pulled out the school's holographic clipboard. He sorted all the different papers then selected the ones that needed to be signed.

"Here, keep the clipboard. We will need some signatures from your parents saying that you will be allowed to work alongside some of the local authorities, as well as permission to teach you defense moves. There are a few lines about not being liable for any bodily injury as well. I have marked all the areas that need signatures. We will be back at the end of the week to pick up the clipboard." Zane handed the clipboard to her, she looked at the page count on the side then sighed.

"I will get my parents to sign it, thanks for coming. Oh, and, Ms Dunlap, if you want your nails a different color just ask."

Gliss smiled and asked for a deep blue. Gliss was admiring her nails as they left the house. Zane was happy to be back in the fresh air. He strapped Gliss in and headed over to Henry's house.

Chapter 12

The Gang

Gliss kept scratching at her nails, Ruby hadn't just painted them she had turned the entire nail the same color. It was a good thing that Gliss liked the color. They had been waiting nearly twenty minutes now for Henry to show up. his mother would periodically appear in the living room to give them updates on the current ETA. Zane and Gliss had assured her that it was all right and that she could tell him they stopped by. After all, it was Henry's mother that was in charge of reading and signing the paperwork. Gliss was about to turn to Zane to ask him about her nails when she was interrupted by loud, exciting music.

Four teenagers strode into the room and the music grew louder, it wasn't unbearable, but the music was a strange addition to the room. Gliss looked for the source but couldn't quite place it. She was surprised to find the music resonating from somewhere around the young man with blonde hair and blue eyes. He wore a shirt with a monster truck on it, and the words

"Monster Jam" written in green oozing letters that seemed to drip onto the truck, coating it with a greenish mud.

"My mom said you were looking for us?" the boy asked.

"Yes, are you Henry? And is that music coming from you?" Zane asked.

"Yes, and yes, who are you?"

Gliss answered, "I am Ms Dunlap, and this is Mr Whitlock, we are here to get a head start on some paperwork that we need from you to participate fully in the Heroes Course this year."

"So, are you going to be like my teachers? You look kind of young and unqualified, no offense," he said, raising both hands in the air in front of him. Gliss felt like he had just slapped her across the face. Who gave him the right to judge whether or not they were qualified to teach even if she knew deep down that they were not?

"You want to see my qualifications? Why don't you step into the ring with me; I bet you don't last two minutes," Gliss snapped back.

Henry looked taken back but then looked her up and down, grinned then said, "Let's do it. Will my back yard suffice?" Henry challenged.

Zane leaned in, "Gliss, I don't think it is the best idea to fight our students. Especially in front of their parents."

Gliss stood up and pulled out a clipboard and shoved it towards Henry's mom who had walked in after hearing something about a fight.

"Please sign page thirty-seven, so I can legally teach your son a lesson."

Henry's mom took the clipboard, read the page then without hesitation signed the form. She tried to hand it back to Gliss, but Gliss insisted that she completed the rest of the paperwork.

"Take it out back, while I work in silence on the rest of the forms." Henry's mom leaned in close so that only Gliss heard the next words.

"Kick his butt for me, I need something embarrassing to tell Lary."

She winked and jerked a thumb towards the sliding glass door. The group moved as one and squeezed out the door after Gliss and Henry. Gliss pulled on her helmet and took a couple steps back facing Henry who stood with arms crossed in defiance. Zane stood on the same side as Gliss but the others in the gang stood and cheered for Henry.

"So, how do you want to do this?" Henry yelled across to her.

"Zane, set a ten second timer. When the timer rings, we start the fight."

"Sounds fair enough, can we use our powers or not?" Henry asked.

Gliss glanced towards Zane who shrugged and looked around at the houses that stood closer than was comfortable with her glitter blast.

"I guess that is fine since we should be learning about what powers you have, but I must warn you that if I use my power, you might be in for a lot of clean up." Gliss said.

The words 'clean up' seemed to be having an unnerving effect on Henry.

"What do you mean... 'clean up'?" Henry asked some of his fire fading,

"I can't tell you that, it would be an unfair advantage. I've given you all the information I can. Are you backing out?" Gliss replied, taunting him.

"Come on, Henry, you can take a little girl," a short blonde kid said, trying to reassure his friend. A girl with long brown hair and bright blue eyes also voiced her support. Soon the whole gang began to reassure their friend. Henry regained his confidence and Zane set a timer.

Gliss watched as the seconds ticked down. A loud bass drum heartbeat with dissonant high-pitched strings added extra tension to the moment and everyone was on edge. The music grew louder and edgier as the bass drum heartbeat slowed the last five seconds. Bmm... bmm. By the time the clock hit two seconds, the music was so loud that most of the others had stepped back away from the two gladiators.

Gliss smiled and was thankful for all the years she spent listening to her music way too loud. The clock hit one second and the music stopped, bringing a tense deafening silence. The timer beeped. Instantly epic action music filled the backyard, loud enough to shake the house windows. Gliss welcomed the epic sounding music and let two spheres drop into both hands.

Gliss was the first to take the offensive. She darted forward into the raging melody. Gliss was on him in an instant. She saw the shock that registered on his face as she reached him and swept his legs out from under him. Henry fell defenseless but Gliss decided to show off her power anyway. She smashed a sphere down onto his chest then dove away, and came rolling to her feet, a couple of yards away. Gliss smiled as she watched the glitter bomb go off. The music took on a panicked tone as Henry and his friends began to be engulfed in an Olympic swimming pool volume of glitter. To her amazement, the glitter blew away in large waves that corresponded with the frantic beat of the music. The pink glitter snowed from the sky as Gliss darted back in and put Henry in a headlock, with his hands stuck behind his back.

Gliss was declared the winner of the fight and the music slowly transitioned to a sad and reminiscent melody that made Zane think of fallen soldiers and epic battles long ago. Henry kept his distance from Gliss as they walked back inside the home. A wide grin spread across Henry's mom's face. She quietly thanked Gliss and returned the signed clipboard.

"So, are you excited for the upcoming school year?" Zane asked. Henry wouldn't meet his eyes but nodded his head.

"So, who are your friends?" Zane asked, trying to change the subject.

"This is RoseAnne, the Growing Rose for short," Henry pointed to the brown-haired girl who sat to his right.

"This guy over here is Logan 'The Pebble' Gardener." He jerked his head to the right towards the shorter blonde-haired kid, "this is Calvin, 'Laser Pointer' Smith."

"Wait, are all of you enrolled in our class?" Zane asked, confused.

"Yeah, that's right," Henry said as the others nodded their heads in agreement.

"Great! Take home these clipboards and sign all the papers then we will be back in a week to collect them. If anyone does not get the paperwork filled out by then they will have to fight Ms Dunlap," Zane said with a flicker of a smile. He handed out the clipboards and together they exited the house.

Gliss looked around the neighborhood and was pleased to find glitter stuck to absolutely everything.

"Well, I think that sums up our list. Let's check in with the dean and Zack to see how things went with them." Gliss agreed and Zane dialed them up as they took off towards the sky. Zane merged the call so that way Gliss could take part in the conversation as well.

"Hello, this is Dean Richardson." came the familiar voice over the line.

"Hello," both Zane and Gliss said in unison.

"Oh, it is just you two. How did it go with your students?"

"It went fine, we got all the paperwork out to the students."

"That's good to hear. We had some trouble reaching Simon but eventually his mother gave us permission to break down his door, to gain access to the room. I have received notice that two new students have been added to the class roster. If you don't mind, could you go meet with them and get the paperwork going?"

"Sure, send over the names and addresses?" Zane said, trying to mask his exhaustion. Gliss could clearly hear it though.

"Great, thank you both. Good luck! See you tonight for dinner."

The dean hung up and a moment later the text came through with the names and addresses. Gliss looked at the names; James Calvier, and Ethan Brite. Gliss tried to talk to Zane but, once again, she found herself left alone to her own thoughts. She waited for what seemed an hour before Zane came on over the communications line.

"Sorry, I am just so tired," Zane said sleepily

"I know, but it is your own fault. You were the one who decided to stay up all night. If you fall asleep while we are in the sky, I will kill you." Gliss threatened.

"I won't fall asleep. I will be fine but, this time, promise me that you won't try and fight the students."

"I can't promise that. What if they need me to teach them a lesson? It would make me a bad teacher to dismiss the needs of my students" Gliss retorted.

"Fine, but let me try to talk with them first."

"All right, but if someone needs a lesson I won't hesitate. Mrs Landreaux appreciated it. She even thanked me."

They landed at a small black house. Zane unclipped Gliss and she shot off towards the door. Gliss pressed the doorbell and waited eagerly for someone to answer. Zane slowly made his way up to her, the door opened and a tall, pale, gangly boy with sunken eyes and black hair stepped out, joining them on the porch.

"Can I help you?" he asked, his voice reminded Gliss of a snake, he almost hissed the words at them.

"Are you James Calvier?"

"Yeah."

"Great, we are teachers from Eastside. We were informed that you have joined the Hero course."

"So?"

"Well, we have some paperwork that we need you and your parents to fill out and get back to us so you can participate in the class this year."

"All right, I will get them signed," he said.

"Great, do you mind if we ask you what your power is?" Gliss asked as she handed him a clipboard. Zane pulled out his notepad.

"Mushrooms and compost. I can turn trash or other things into either mushrooms or compost."

"Interesting," Gliss heard Zane whisper under his breath.

"Is there anything else you want to ask me?" James asked. Neither Gliss nor Zane had any further questions and they waved goodbye. James slunk back into the confines of his house.

"That kid gave me the creeps," Gliss said to Zane.

"Na, I think he is a lot nicer than he looks or sounds. Just misunderstood," Zane said.

Gliss thought about it, and she felt bad she had called him creepy. Zane was probably right; James was most likely a very nice kid.

"Zane, I just remembered that we forgot to ask the other kids about their powers."

"You're right... I guess we'll just have to wait to find out," Zane said as they soared over the city.

Ethan Brite was the shiniest person Gliss had ever met and his entire room was covered in mirrors. Ethan was tall and well-built. His face was very attractive, with high cheekbones and a sturdy chin. He had dark brown eyes, but his whole look was overwhelmed by the sheer amount of mirrors he had strapped to his body. Ethan explained that he could walk through mirrors to connecting ones around the house or surrounding area. He demonstrated by walking through a tall mirror that hung from his wall and emerged from a closet on the opposite side of the house.

Zane had to drag Gliss from the house. Gliss, in turn, spent the rest of the flight refusing Zane's communication requests. The conversation at dinner was not as fun as they had expected it to be. It was dry and uncomfortable. So much so, that Zane actually fell asleep at the dinner table. Gliss said good night and caught a cab home. She spent the rest of the night fidgeting with her sheets, pillows, and blankets, trying to get comfortable. The night yielded little sleep to her, or her mother, and she felt more empathy towards Zane's sleeplessness.

Chapter 13

First Day of Class

Zane woke up from what was probably the best sleep that he'd had over the summer break. It had been a particularly cool evening and it had been stress-free as he had shared the evening with his parents and Gliss. Zane smiled as he rose from his bunker of blankets. He walked into the living room and used the end of a broom to wake up Zack from inside his mound of clothes. The familiar face appeared moments later and the rare sighting of Zack in his natural environment (a dirty living room) set Zane at peace. Zane walked over to the refrigerator, pulled it open and searched for the breakfast that Gliss had prepared for him the day before. He found it and placed it in the microwave. Zane set the time for a minute thirty then dashed into the bathroom to do his hair and ready himself for the day. Zane smiled at himself in the mirror and was pleased to find not just one but two hairs protruding from his chin. *This would be the year he would grow his beard* he thought to himself.

Zane felt the confidence inside his chest. He was sure it was raging so strong that it was emitting a smell.

Zane remembered the food he had left in the microwave and dashed back into the room to consume his confidence. Confidence never tasted so good.

Zane finished his food and picked out his starched, ironed button-up shirt. It was black, which he had been told on many occasions was a slimming color. Zane came back out into the room. He grabbed his backpack which contained his and Zack's suits. Zack came out of the bathroom and Zane was surprised to find that Zack smelled like flowers, in a good way.

"You ready, bro?" Zack asked, whipping his hair over his shoulder.

"You know it, let's go" Zane said opening the front door. He and Zack made it down to the parking lot. Zane felt comfortable driving with Zack. It had taken a couple of weeks of driving with him to appreciate his skill. When he drove with Zack it gave Zane the realization of just how precious life is. Zane closed his door and immediately put on his seatbelt. The car chimed, informing Zack that he had not put on his seat belt. Zack did not put his seatbelt on but instead, as they drove, he would yell at the top of his lungs each time it would come on.

They arrived at the school and Zane was full of gratitude as he stepped out onto the pavement. Zane walked towards the school that he had attended for so many years as a student with different eyes. He now viewed the school as a place of work, a place of learning and molding. Zane pulled up to the large front door with added appreciation and he felt pride swell inside his chest as he swiped his key card granting him access to the building. Zane stepped into his new future. The lights above flickered slightly as he entered, giving the moment a dramatic effect. Zane turned his head and found the source that was causing the unusual light effect. Dean Richardson strode towards them. He wore a blue and black pinstripe suit. His eyebrows were unusually low, they sunk down and even covered a portion of his nose.

Usually, Zane would have cowered from the gaze of the large man but, after getting to know him over the summer, Zane stood his ground.

"Good morning, Dean Richardson," Zane said as he passed. Zane did not get a response.

"He is just nervous for the first day of school, he usually takes a couple weeks to relax." Mr Thorne said from behind them. Zane turned and looked at his past teacher.

"Good morning, Mr Thorne. It's good to see you."

"Yeah… it's good to see you too. Now, if you don't mind, I have to get to the faculty lounge to see what kind of bagels the administration bought this year."

"Right, sorry," Zane said, stepping aside so the little man could pass.

"Zack, are you ready for today? I am beginning to feel a little nervous. What if the kids don't listen?"

"Don't sweat it, bro. I didn't listen to my teachers and look how I turned out. I can handle anything these kids can dish out. Besides, today we will be together to teach; not that reading disclosures is doing much teaching. Tomorrow will be much harder," Zack said, trying to reassure Zane but the words only made him feel even more concerned. His stomach felt as if it were filled with a churning tornado of butterflies. Maybe it was just his confidence. In defiance of fear or indigestion, they made their way to the classroom and Zane was relieved to find Gliss waiting inside.

"Good morning, coworkers!" Gliss said beaming. She smiled and her radiant mood re-established his confidence.

"'Morning," Zack said, making his way over to a corner where he had arranged three desks together to form one large one. Zack unzipped his backpack and pulled out a laser engraved gold plaque with the title, 'Mr Zack, Teacher of Chill and Respect'. He centered the plaque on his central desk, then took a seat and leaned back against the wall, humming to himself quietly. Zane walked over and joined Gliss at the front of the classroom. She was fidgeting with a blue ribbon that was dangling from her braid.

"Are you ready for this?" Zane asked, stepping in closer to examine the braid.

"Of course, I'm ready. Did you remember to send out disclosures to all the students this morning?" she asked him.

"Yes, I did it last night, so hopefully some of them got them signed."

"Zane, we are talking about sixteen-year-olds. I don't think a single one of them spent the last day of summer filling out disclosure documents."

"You never know, maybe that James kid got his papers signed; he looked responsible."

"If anyone did, Ethan got his signed," Gliss replied as she got a far off look in her eye. Zane felt jealousy rising in his chest. Gliss had never said his name and got that look before. So, Zane did the only thing he could think of to turn her focus back on him; Zane leaned in and kissed Gliss good morning.

Gliss pulled back then smiled and said, "I've been waiting for my good morning kiss." Zane was happy that his move had worked.

Gliss pulled the ribbon from her hair and with a groan dismissed herself to the bathroom to redo her braid. Zane occupied himself by rearranging the seating chart. He moved Ethan to the back of the room. The rest of the students were all seated in the front of the classroom. Zane thought that the extra five rows of empty desks would do nicely. Zane dropped the classroom tablet as his diabolical plan was disrupted by the appearance of their first student.

A tall, muscle-bound Polynesian kid walked in through the door. He wore a bright yellow shirt, with blinding fluorescent green shorts. He had deep brown eyes, and Zane was surprised to see a goatee sprouting from a proud chin.

"What's up, homie?" the intimidating young man said to Zane and Zack as he took a seat at the back of the room.

"Hey, man, you can call me Zack. It's nice to meet you," Zack said, walking over and performing some kind of secret handshake that was only taught to a select few cool kids.

"The name's Simon."

"All right, I feel you, bro. Sick kicks you got," Zack replied. Zane stood back and watched the whole encounter with awe. Zane didn't really understand what was going on but somehow Zack had just gained the respect of their senior.

"Hey, Simon, it's nice to meet you. I am Mr Whitlock. You know you're five minutes early, right?"

"Nice to meet you too, Mr Whitlock. I know. I like to warm up my seat for five minutes before class begins."

"Oh. Well, I have the seating chart if you would like to see your seat." Zane offered.

"Na, I think I will sit here for a bit, I will let you know if I choose to move somewhere else," Simon responded with a genuine smile.

Zane had never encountered this kind of resistance, he actually had never experienced any resistance. Zane didn't know whether he should try to force his class rules right away or ease into them. The conflict inside him began to build. Gliss walked back into the room and Zane immediately walked over to her and pulled her out into the hallway. Zane let out a breath and Gliss looked worried.

"Zane, is something wrong?" Gliss asked, placing one hand on his shoulder. Zane took a minute and explained what had happened to him while she was gone.

"Zane, it's fine, we don't have a lot of students. I feel like we kind of need to bend rather than be more rigid. I know you like your rules. But we only have one shot at this, and the faster we gain the respect and appreciation of our students, the better we can help them to shape their future," Gliss finished and gave him a hug before dancing around him into the classroom to introduce herself to Simon.

Zane stood out the hallway letting the words swirl inside his brain until the bell rang. He knew that Gliss was right about this. Zane told himself that he would be more bendable. He walked into the classroom and took his place alongside Gliss at the front of the room. The students all funneled in and Gliss activated the seating chart. To Zane's amusement he watched as Ethan saw his name, looked towards Zane then clenched his jaw and took a seat next to Simon. Zane at least liked to think he looked at him. Zane glanced at the student who was sitting in front of him. Henry Landrioux sat with his feet kicked up on the desk and leaned back lackadaisically.

Gliss frowned, as she noticed Ethan sitting at the back of the room. She glanced up at the seating chart. It was as clear as day that she did not approve of Zane's impulsive action. She gave him an icy glare and Zane swallowed hard. The intercom buzzed and to Zane's relief the dean's voice came online.

"Good morning, students! We are happy to have you here; this is going to be a great year. We have some exciting new programs, and some very fun activities planned for the coming year. I just wanted to say: let's make this the best year the school has seen yet. We are surrounded by some of the best and brightest minds."

Zane noted more than one scoff at the claim from his students.

"I know that we have had some rumors circulating about the reasons for Mrs McCoy's absence this year. May I give some peace as I tell you that she felt that she had another calling in life other than being a teacher and she left to pursue her other aspirations and dreams. That is all. Have a wonderful day."

The intercom cut off and the normal sounds of students playing on their phones and not paying attention took over the room. There was also the abnormal sound of orchestral music playing a pleasant but uninteresting melody very quietly. Zane looked at Gliss for some help, but she was too busy avoiding him.

"Welcome class I am Mr Whitlo…" Zane was cut off as Henry shouted.

"We know who you are. When are we going to get to pick out our suits?"

All the other students grunted or voiced their agreement. Zane was finding that he was not being a very good teacher, as widespread conversation began about Zane being a baby teacher who was afraid of everything. Something snapped inside Zane, all flexibility that he had promised Gliss was fleeing from within him, like a shadow being chased down by the sun to find hiding places behind buildings, or under trash bins.

"That is enough! The next person who speaks will not only be sent to the dean's office but will not be getting a suit," Zane said all, skittishness banished from his being. Conversation ended abruptly and Zane took charge of his classroom.

"If you really want to know when you will be getting suits or anything about this class, then you should have read the disclosures that you all signed apparently without reading. It clearly outlines a timeline for the class; what will be covered and what will not be tolerated. I will not speak another word until each and every one of you has read the disclosure so we can get all the stupid questions and notions out of the way before they are voiced in this classroom," Zane said ruthlessly. He didn't even make eye-contact with his co-teachers because Zane found the very thought of his colleagues infuriating.

Phones came out and the disclosure was accessed by every student. Zane walked over to his desk and sat down gazing over his students who were now reading the thirty-five paged, very detailed disclosure.

Zane began to think about what he would have done in this very situation as a student. He would have skimmed the majority of the papers picking out key details. Then he would have spent the remainder of the class doodling or forgetting the information he had just input into his brain. The thought led Zane to think about what he would have thought about himself as a teacher, Zane grimaced as he realized that he would have hated himself as a teacher. When Gliss approached his desk, she did so hesitantly and stood a couple feet away, as if Zane had some disease that she could catch if she got too close. Zane sighed then stood up and walked from the room. Gliss followed behind him like a lost puppy. Before exiting the room, he told the students that Zack 'Teacher of Chill and Respect' was in charge. Zack nodded to Zane in a relaxed way as he walked out of the room.

When he was sure that they were far enough away from the class to not be heard, he stopped and waited for the fiery darts to be let loose on him from behind. They never came. Instead, a tight hug enveloped him from behind. Gliss's face pressed into his back and her arms wrapped around his stomach. They stood that way for a long time, neither of them speaking. The hug ended as shouts erupted from their class behind them.

Gliss said, "Let's get back, you don't have to teach any more today. Let me teach today and tomorrow you and Zack can team teach."

Zane let the animosity fade from inside of him leaving him in a gray mood, drained of emotion, Zane felt like a deflating balloon as Gliss towed him back to the room.

"Thanks, Gliss," he said just before they noticed the chaos. The room was on fire. The steel door wouldn't budge, barring the exit from the room. Zane looked at the scene inside the room with horror. He saw panic-stricken faces as a group of students tried to break out of the barred windows. Smoke was billowing from the seams at the door.

"Zane, get the dean now! I'm going to try to break in," Gliss said. She began setting up some Glitter charges, as Zane fell towards the floor then shot off. He scraped an elbow on the wall as he turned down the hallway. Zane pushed his body as fast as the compact space would allow.

It was the fastest he had ever flown indoors. Zane didn't stop when a door appeared. Instead, he turned his body and hit the door feet-first. The door flew off its hinges and Zane's knees and feet hurt from the impact. Zane braced himself for the second door as he noticed the shocked face of Gliss's aunt. Zane broke the second door down and stopped as he saw the dean holding the desk over his head ready to throw it at Zane. The dean stopped in mid-throw and set the desk down hard instead.

"What in the blue blazes is going on?" he asked worriedly.

"Our classroom is on fire and our students are locked inside. We need your help to break down the door," Zane said the last words, ending abruptly as he ran out of breath. The dean didn't waste a second. He bolted past Zane, shoving him aside as he rushed through the front office.

"Marge, call nine-one-one; we have an emergency. Zane, try to get Mr Thorne to the room as quickly as possible."

Merely Justice exited the room. Marge picked up the phone and began to dial the fire department. Zane whizzed out of the room and flew down a hallway opposite the dean. Zane found his old teacher in the middle of a lecture. Zane rushed in and, without explaining a thing, grabbed Mr Thorne under the armpits despite his protests. The little man was carried at blinding speed down the hallways of the school.

Chapter 14

Fiery Consequences

Gliss watched her students struggling, with terror. She cursed herself for not being inside with them. Glitter was now up to her waist and the door had not budged. No matter where she cracked a sphere, it did not have an impact on the door. Gliss wondered how long it would take to get the dean. It must have already been six or seven minutes. Gliss looked in and watched as the students gathered together, forming some kind of resistance to the fire. The walls and ceilings were changing color at a blinding speed. This stopped as Gliss watched Henry yell something at Ruby, who stopped and joined the group. RoseAnne stepped forward and pressed a hand to the carpet. A wall of thick vines shot up from the floor and separated the flames from the students. Zack rushed over to the door and pressed his hand against it. Gliss felt as the door began to vibrate. Beads of sweat formed on Zack's forehead as he forced his hand to vibrate faster. Nothing happened. Zack made eye contact with Gliss, and he looked scared. Gliss pointed a finger at the students then mouthed the words, "work together to get out, my spheres aren't doing anything."

Zack nodded his head and ran back to the students. A minute later, Logan walked up to the door, and pulled out a small tube of, what looked like, rocks and sand. He downed the contents with a painful swallow and Gliss watched as he grew to a monstrous size. His muscles bulged and his shirt ripped off his body as his head touched the ceiling. Veins popped out on every part of his body. Logan a.k.a. "The Pebble" attacked the door furiously. Gliss stepped back as she watched the frame shake and dust fall from the surrounding wall, but that was all that the attack did.

"Such a shame that you weren't in there too. Let me guess, you sent Zane away? I was hoping to enjoy the show by myself, but I guess your company will suffice. We can watch them all die. None of their powers are strong enough to escape. You're all weak and that includes you, Ms Dunlap."

Jane McCoy stepped up beside Gliss, her heels clicking on the cement floor. Gliss turned to her.

"Mrs McCoy, what did you do?"

"Me? I didn't do anything, but I think you will be surprised when you find out who did do this."

Gliss gritted her teeth.

"You have to help me save them! You would have to be a monster to stand by and watch innocent children die!"

"I'm not going to stand by. Why would you ever think that? No, I think revenge sounds sweeter to me."

She said with an eerie smile. Gliss lunged at her former teacher and found herself smashing into the wall a moment later. Gliss reeled back cradling an injured wrist.

"You missed me, deeay. You're going to have to do better than that!" Mrs McCoy said, while rubbing her forefinger and thumb together inspecting a piece of glitter. Gliss bent down and pulled a couple spheres from her shoe compartments.

Instead of getting close this time, Gliss hurled a sphere at Mrs McCoy. Gliss was knocked backwards by an explosion of glitter. *Had her own sphere hit her in the chest? She* thought to herself, as she tumbled backwards down the hallway.

She came to a stop as she collided with a set of lockers which looked familiar to her. She recognized them as the lockers that she had been given to use. Quickly, Gliss stood and opened the locker containing her suit. She noticed blood seeping from a cut on her knee. Gliss hurriedly pulled on the suit, she locked her helmet into place and the interface lit up.

"New suit? I like the colors. You were one of my favorite pupils. I don't think that is going to help you though. Go ahead and try it."

Gliss broke the spheres in her boots and the pressure gauge began to climb. The display showed that she had forty-eight unused spheres left. Gliss took aim, then fired. It sounded like a gun as she pulled back from the recoil. This time glitter did not explode around her and Gliss found herself smiling as she watched Mrs

McCoy skid down the hallway. Gliss sprinted towards Jane. She decided that Jane did not deserve the title of Mrs McCoy. Anyone who threatened children and enjoyed it, lost their ability to love, along with their humanity. For now, the monster in front of her would be called Jane.

Gliss stopped midway down the hall, as Ethan fell out of a small mirror attached to one of the lockers. He slumped forward and Gliss knelt down to check on him.

"Ethan, are you all right?" she asked,

"It's Mirrious, not Ethan, we are heroes now."

"Okay, whatever, are you all right? Has anyone else managed to escape?" Ethan shook his head. Gliss noticed the knife out of the corner of her eye. She shoved Ethan to the side and dove towards the opposite wall. Gliss watched as the weapon skidded away down the hall, then watched as it melted into the floor and re-appeared in Jane's hand.

"Ethan, get out of here and go find the dean!" Gliss yelled "It's Mirrious!" he shouted as he dove through a pocket mirror that he had dropped on the ground.

"You don't actually think he can leave to find the dean, right? Haven't you wondered why it is taking Zane so long to get back here? You will have to thank my brother. Some of his victims are still stuck in alternate sub-dimensions he left them in. No one is coming to save you, or your students."

Gliss watched as the knife spun through the air once more. This time Gliss did something completely reckless. She dodged the knife but dove backwards to avoid getting impaled. The knife landed only a couple of feet away. Gliss took aim with her arm and fired a sphere just as the knife was melting into the floor. She watched as the gooey-looking floor absorbed her shot. Gliss stood up and raced forward. Glitter exploded from Jane which shoved her off-balance. Gliss took advantage of the moment and grabbed the knife from Jane's hand, as she toppled over. Gliss quickly turned around and pressed the knife up against the side of Jane's neck.

"Don't even think about moving. If you even so much as flinch I won't hesitate. Before you try to portal me somewhere else, I will make sure you're dead," Gliss hissed in her ear. Gliss thought about the words she had used; most of them directly from one of her favorite crime TV shows. She decided it didn't feel right to say, but it was too late to take the words back.

"What do you want? Do you want your students to be freed? Or do you want Zane back? I will only let you pick one. What will it be, Glissandra?" Gliss's heart sank as she tried to imagine the rest of her life without Zane. No matter how hard it hurt she knew that her students came first.

"Let my students go," Gliss said.

"As you wish." Jane began to melt from underneath Gliss, but Gliss rammed the knife forward as she began to ooze away. The knife slid through the area where a neck used to be and Gliss cursed as it came away clean.

She hurled the knife down the hallway. Gliss was ready to scream as her frustration swelled within her. She ran back to the door. The whole frame shook then tore clean away from the wall. Her students came pouring out into the hallway, Gliss ran forward and helped Zack to his feet, his face was covered in ash and his breathing was shallow and ragged.

Mirrious fell from the ceiling once again, landing hard. The rest of the class ran over to greet him. He stood up then walked over to join Gliss and Zack.

"I looked everywhere. There was no sign of the dean, Zane, or anyone else in the school. It's as if they've vanished."

Gliss kept her helmet on as she began to cry; she didn't want her students to see her like this.

"Come on kids, let's get out of here; many of you have burns that will need to be checked out by the paramedics. I am sorry that I wasn't in there with you guys." She looked around at the solemn group. A soft sad melody began to play behind them as they made their way through the glitter-filled hallways.

"So, how did you guys get out of there anyway? Oh, and how did the fire start?" Gliss asked, Ruby spoke up and began to tell the story.

"Well, we were all just sitting there in class reading as Mr Witlock had instructed us to do. When you guys walked out, we decided to take a break. Mr Zack told us a crazy story about Mr Whitlock, then, out of nowhere this tall man with red skin and dark blue eyes came out of the ceiling. He laughed and set the room on fire, then he dropped through the floor like he was made of some kind of goop."

"I was the first to yell fire," RoseAnne interrupted.

"As I was saying, when we realized the room was on fire, we tried to exit, but for some reason the computer locked down the room with us still inside. Zack tried to cut one of the fire sprinkler lines but the line was completely empty. That was when panic broke out," Ruby said, pausing for dramatic effect.

"All right, all right, you're taking too long to tell the story. It's my turn to finish," Henry said, shoving Ruby out of the way.

"Ruby lost her cool and began to change everything in sight to a different color, so I took command and told her if she changed my shoe color one more time, I would throw her in the fire myself. So, Roseanne separated us from the fire, and we each tried our hand at opening the door. It wasn't until we realized that Ethan could leave and open the door from the outside that real progress was made. Once the pretty boy left, all the girls' brains began to work and we realized that our boy, James, could turn any organic structure into compost, which is what RoseAnne needs to make her plants. So, working together, with the help of the Pebble to break all the desks into pieces, Mycelious then turned everything into compost. I came up with the name because the kid really likes mushrooms."

James nodded his agreement at the new nickname. "The Growing Rose stepped in and, with her vine power, ripped the door right out of the wall. That's when we escaped," he finished up and everyone nodded in agreement.

Gliss wondered after hearing the story from Henry if, he was actually a member of the mob crime families. She thought about the threat he had thrown at Ruby and then remembered she had listened to him without a second thought. Gliss was probably blowing things out of proportion. She couldn't help but notice Zane's backpack before they exited the building. She reached down and grabbed it. This would be the last thing of his she would ever open. She couldn't find the strength to look through his things. So, instead, she just embraced the backpack. Gliss took one last walk around the school searching for any clues as to the whereabouts of the missing student and faculty population. She couldn't find anything that even stuck out to her as odd or peculiar.

She sighed then with all the courage she could muster, walked over to the front door, then pulled the fire alarm. The lights came on and the alarms sounded. Her students sat or laid on the grass out front and just breathed. Zack had recovered some of his strength and his breaths were now coming in much easier. He walked up alongside her and pulled out his phone.

"Gliss, you might want to sit down before you watch this. We might also want to think about getting out of town."

The other buildings were now emptying of students and teachers to see what all the noise was about. Zack held his phone up so that she could see the screen. He used his finger to tap the small triangular shaped 'play' button on the screen.

The video began to play. Gliss sucked in a sharp breath. There was no audio, but the video was time-stamped and showed Zane and Gliss sneaking into the school. The camera zoomed in on their faces. The time-stamp was last night. The cameras transitioned as Zane and Gliss entered the building and followed them down to the classroom where Zane pulled off the wall panel leading into their classroom. He began to clip wires and Gliss watched the uncanny person portraying herself step into the classroom. The video continued and Gliss watched as her doppelganger emptied the fire sprinkler system. The video cut to the most recent footage of the classroom in flames and the students fighting for their lives. There was a clip of Gliss fighting, not Jane, but a police officer. All the blood drained from Gliss's face as she realized how this all looked. Zack pulled the phone away and stowed it back in his hoodie.

"Listen, that's not me. Zane and I were at our parents' houses last night. Also, you know that there was no police officer."

"I know. One of my hobbies is tracking people's cell phones. My uncle has kept tabs on both of you since you signed on. I found this video playing on every major news station. We need to leave now," Zack hissed at her.

191

Gliss didn't know what to do. She felt like she should fight this, then realized that the people who had the power and influence to accomplish this probably had the means to squash her until she spent the rest of her life behind bars.

"Okay, let's go.''

Zack began to lead them away. Gliss stopped then ran back to their class. Fire burned inside most of their eyes. She found Ethan, ran up to him. He looked conflicted.

"Mirrious, you know that Zane and I didn't do this. I need your help to convince the others. You know who I was fighting in the hallway. I know you know because I can see it in your eyes.

When the time's right I will contact you, until then please try to help the others understand."

He didn't look at her right away but, when he did, she knew that he believed her.

"Leavin' so soon. I think you got some explainin' to do," Henry said, stepping in front of her.

"Before you tell me that you two didn't do it, save me the tears, sweetheart. Pebble, grab her!"

Logan stepped towards her, but Gliss dove to the right and dodged the mass of muscles. A vine wrapped around one of her legs and Gliss had to stomp with her other foot to break the plant off. Once she was free, she began to run but the sounds of thundering feet pounded behind her. Gliss pulled on her helmet, and she loaded a sphere into place then shot it behind her. Glitter exploded filling the air causing confusion to break out. Gliss found herself flying a moment later; Zack had swooped down wearing his suit. Gliss found the ride uncomfortable, as her teeth chattered with every foot they climbed. Just when Gliss thought they were free from the bombardment of attacks, a laser pointer shined through her visor blinding her. Gliss felt her body begin to drop towards the ground as Zack cried out from above. Gliss's vision cleared, and she watched as the laser pointer continued to follow Zack's evasive maneuvers. Gliss turned her body, so she faced the ground. she spotted the culprit. Calvin 'Laser Pointer' Smith was blinding Zack with his laser pointer vision. Gliss took aim. As she plummeted, she exhaled and fired. She wasn't sure she had hit her target as the force from the shot sent her into a dizzying spiral. Gliss primed her suit to its maximum pressure.

She remembered Zane's instructions on how to fly with her suit or at least glide for a considerable distance. Gliss held her hands out and shouted the command to fly. A sound like a screaming banshee surrounded her. Gliss opened her eyes as she began to level out. She let out her breath as she saw the beauty below. Every color of the rainbow, plus many, many more, shot out cascading below her. Gliss began to pick up speed. Her speedometer showed her accelerating at well over two-hundred miles-an-hour. The city she knew so well passed beneath her feet in a moment. Gliss looked behind her and found that Zack had made it through and was in pursuit. Gliss checked on her pressure and sphere tanks which read ninety-nine percent full. The excitement from the battle and flight kept a steady supply of spheres for the moment. The estimated time she could fly showed a whopping sixty-two hours, assuming her elevated emotional state continued. Gliss was almost tempted to fly for sixty-two hours if it meant flying somewhere where she could disappear from her feelings. Glitter continued to spew out from behind her with a sound like a rocket. As tears began to drip down her face, the glitter jet-trail slowly transitioned to deep blues and blacks.

Snapping out of most of her sorrow, Gliss found herself face-to -face with the blue mountains that had looked so small her entire life. They loomed before her looking daunting and immovable. She would either have to land or begin to climb steeply. Gliss wondered why Zack hadn't caught up to her yet. She risked a glance behind to find him a speck in the distance. Gliss eased the pressure and slowed down to allow Zack to catch up to her. When he did, he motioned to the knob on her helmet. Gliss twisted it and Zack's voice came online.

"Wow, girl! That was faster than most recreational aircraft! You have to get your Flyer License! Yo, anyway, Gliss, where are you going? You should probably land and let me fly you the rest of the way unless you want them to find us by the end of the night. You're not leaving breadcrumbs, but I think that this is a little easier to follow."

"I don't know where I am going! I just wanted to fly away so I could leave my problems behind," she said a little too snappishly. She sighed "sorry. You are right. I will land on the hill over there."

Gliss pointed a finger at a small grassy knoll that rose up out of a farmer's field. She changed her trajectory and initiated the landing sequence. She landed in a wave of glitter and Zack landed beside her.

"Don't worry, Gliss. My uncle will find a way to locate us."

"I don't think you understand, Zack. When I told everyone that the rest of the school had evacuated, I lied."

"When I was fighting with Jane McCoy, she told me that her brother trapped Zane and your uncle in some kind of alternate sub-dimension. She mentioned that some of his victims still haven't found their way out. I'm not sure that it is something your uncle and Zane can just walk away from. I fear they might be gone forever," Gliss said, dropping her head as she said the last word.

"Wow! That's some heavy stuff. Don't worry, my uncle has faced much harder things in his days being a hero. They will be back before you know it. Let's get going. I have a place we can hide out until we figure out what to do. I have a friend who raises alpacas a couple hours away, who would be more than happy to let us crash with him."

With that Gliss found herself vibrating away through the sky. When she landed, her arms and legs felt like jello. She found walking difficult. Zack led her up to a round canvas tent. He let out some kind of loud yodel noise and three alpacas came galloping around the side of the tent. They walked up to Zack and began to nuzzle him. A second yodel came from the depths of the tent, which Gliss thought was called a yurt. A tall man with dark skin and black long hair twisted into the same snake-like tendrils as Zack's came from within the tent.

"Zack, it is my pleasure to find you at my gates, and who is this fine young lady in our midst?" he asked in a deep resonating voice.

"Reggie, brother, this is a friend of mine, Gliss. She and her boyfriend are feeling some heat right now. We are in need of a place to lie low for a while."

"My home is your hiding place. Welcome, Zack, I trust you can show your friend around the farm? You will be working the triple-pass tomorrow. I have lost three alpacas this week up there and I require assistance."

"Of course, we would be happy to assist you." Zack gave a slight bow, and Reggie returned the bow then retreated into his yurt. Zack led them down a path. The three alpacas from earlier returned and guided them down to four other smaller yurts.

"I will take the one on the left. It is the one I built. You are welcome to any of the others. If it were me, I would choose the one in the middle. Gentry built that one. She wouldn't mind if you crashed there for a while." Zack walked to his yurt and closed the flap.

Gliss walked to the middle yurt and opened the flap. |Lavish rugs and blankets sat neatly folded in the corner. The softest pillows Gliss had ever felt lay scattered around the floor. She piled them together retrieving the plushest blanket in the world from the stack, then lay down. The tears rolled down her cheeks and her shoulders shook softly as she fell asleep.

Chapter 15

Ghosts

Zane felt like he had flown through a wall of pure nausea. The temporary feeling was enough to make him drop Mr Thorne. Zane watched as the teacher sped away down the polished hallway. Zane ended up hitting a concrete pillar and he heard a popping noise as his shoulder dislocated. Zane shouted as he hit the floor and slid to a spinning stop.

"I do believe there is an explanation in order and let's not forget an apology! Is this some kind of joke?" Mr Thorne said, pulling himself off the ground. Zane whimpered as he tried to use his shoulder to push himself off the dirty floor

"Sorry, Mr Thorne, there was no time to explain. Our students are trapped inside a burning room. Dean Richardson told me to get you to the room as quickly as possible. Now, if you don't mind, we have some rescuing to do," Zane said, pulling himself to his feet.

They did not fly the rest of the way, instead walking briskly. Every step was excruciating for Zane as his arm flopped uselessly at his side. Zane skidded to a halt and Mr Thorne walked into the frozen statue of dean Richardson.

"What on earth? Who placed this statue here?" Mr Thorne complained, rubbing his now red nose. Zane stepped back and poked the statue.

His finger squished slightly as would happen when poking the flesh of another. Zane looked at Mr Thorne and it dawned on him that this was no statue. Upon closer inspection, Zane could see ever so slight chest movements as the dean breathed in and out. Zane snapped back into reality as he remembered the dire situation at hand. He hoped that Gliss had been able to get into the class and free the students. Zane motioned for Mr Thorne to follow him. The little man did not move at first. He was still frozen inspecting the statue.

"Come on, we have to hurry!" Zane yelled over his shoulder as he began his brisk walk once more. Zane rounded the corner and found a rather unusual scene unfolding in front of him.

He could see Gliss, but it seemed as if there was something wrong with her. Zane watched as she smashed sphere after sphere into the barred door. Zane stepped up to her.

"Gliss, I brought Mr Thorne. We are here to help. What can we do?" Zane asked Gliss who did not move and acted as if he wasn't there at all.

"Gliss!" Zane said, reaching for her hand. Zane nearly died as his hand passed through hers completely. *This is it; I have finally done it. I've died while flying*

Mr Thorne., I must have killed him too. Maybe that was the reason for the nausea, which must be the feeling you have when you retire from mortality and become a ghost. Zane tried over and over to yell her name or just grab her hand one last time. Zane had watched his fair share of movies. He knew this was the time that he would hear the words being whispered, "go into the light."

Zane waited for the famed words, but they did not come. Zane watched as Mrs McCoy walked up and joined Gliss. Zane's blood went cold as he saw the knife tucked into the waistband of his former teacher's belt. Zane screamed and tried to warn Gliss, but it was to no avail. He watched as Gliss attacked and, for a brief second, Gliss was there with him. Zane began to yell but she disappeared before he could get the words out. Zane watched in horror as Gliss threw a sphere at Mrs McCoy. Zane nearly caught it as it whizzed past him and then flashed out to hit Gliss in the chest. Zane watched as she tumbled through the air. He felt hope as he saw her put on the suit he designed.

"Come on, Gliss, use the gun function. It might be the only thing that will keep you safe," Zane said, cheering her on. He shouted with joy as she did just that and watched Mrs McCoy fly backwards. Then Ethan fell out of a locker. Gliss stopped and began to talk with him. Zane watched as Mrs McCoy recovered and pulled the knife out and threw it at Gliss.

"No! Watch out, Gliss!'' Zane yelled. He almost felt as if she heard him as she dove away. Zane watched as the knife clattered to the floor. Then he watched the same knife shimmer and fly past him. Zane watched as it reappeared in Mrs McCoy's hand. *That's my ticket back to the world of the living. All I have to do is catch a ride with the knife the next time it passes through.*

Zane thought to himself. Zane went and stood where Gliss was. He waited for the moment and tensed as it came. The knife spun through the air and Zane backed away behind Gliss. Zane readied himself for the moment. The knife began to shimmer just as Zane was about to grab it. Gliss fired a sphere at the knife that sent it sputtering away from Zane's grasp. Before Zane could reach it, the knife was gone; not tangible to him in its ghostly form. Zane watched as the glitter sphere sent Mrs McCoy falling to her right. Zane watched, holding his breath, as Gliss pressed the knife to Mrs McCoy' s throat. Zane stumbled back as Mrs McCoy became a ghost herself. She opened her eyes then a wry smile spread across her face.

"I was hoping to catch you here. Too bad about your shoulder. Don't worry. I'm not going to fight you. Zane, I didn't know that your girlfriend had it in her, but I was surprised when she threatened to kill me. A silly sentiment but I could see the coldness in those eyes."

"What did you do to me, Mrs McCoy?" Zane asked, trying to forget the poison that was spewing from her mouth.

"It's 'Jane', sweetie. Don't worry, if you're good I might decide to let her see you again before I kill her. That won't be for a while. I honestly didn't mean to bring you and Glissandra into this mess, but when you got in my way, I had no choice. Merely Justice deserved what he got but, this time, I won't let him get away. The world will be better off in my care than his anyway," She said while strolling down the hallway.

"Let me go!" Zane demanded. She stopped short, then turned, looking him up and down.

"no one tells me what to do. If you don't shut your mouth right now, I could easily make this dagger slip into her dimension and find its way to her heart," Jane said, twirling the gleaming weapon. To prove her point she walked over to where Gliss crouched and positioned the dagger at her chest.

"It's your choice; either pick your life or hers." Zane forgot about the pain that he felt in his shoulder. He rushed towards Jane. She danced away from him. Zane attempted a second attack but was met with the same outcome.

"Well, it's been fun talking, but I have other plans to put in motion. Have a nice life, Zane" Jane disappeared leaving Zane alone. He followed Gliss for the remainder of the day. He watched as she tried to keep it together. The worst part of the day was watching the horrible video that made them out to be villains. He was proud of his students, as he watched them work together to try to stop Gliss, but he was also worried, as they fought to stop her. Zane flew with Zack and Gliss. Well, he tried to, at least. Zane followed in the jet stream of Glitter. It took him two hours to cover the distance she did in less than thirty minutes. Zane felt pride as he watched his hard work function so much better than he had anticipated. Zane followed the trail of glitter to a grassy knoll where it abruptly ended. He had to rack his brain as to where they could have possibly gone. It wasn't until Zane remembered Zack telling him about some alpaca farm he used to live in the mountains, that Zane understood. He searched for hours before he found the place.

Zane would have never found it if he hadn't seen Zack walking out of some yurt in the forest. Zane searched the yurt and regretted it immediately, as he saw the pile of laundry that looked as if it were growing fungus inside the tent. Zane found the middle yurt and was happy to see Gliss lying inside. He watched as she cried. All he wanted to do was hug her and tell her it was going to be all right. Zane cried himself to sleep too. It was the loneliest he had ever felt.

The night was cold and the ground hard and unforgiving. Zane shivered as a breeze blew through the now-opened tent flap. He sat up and rubbed his eyes, then rolled to his knees and stood up. Stretching as he made his way out of the yurt, Zane walked down the pathway searching for Gliss. He continued to walk for some time. He found himself staring at one of the alpacas. It stared back at him. Zane veered off the pathway giving the creature room. The animal followed his movement. Zane froze then addressed the animal.

"You can see me?" he asked, walking closer to the fuzzy animal. The alpaca watched him with interested eyes. Zane reached out a hand and to his amazement Zane felt the animal, unlike with Gliss or the other things he had interacted with, he actually felt the soft fur. Zane nearly cried as he felt the tangible curls between his fingers. Zane ran back to the yurts. He was happy to find Zack still sleeping, Zane reached out a hand and tried to shake his friend. Once again, his hand passed through as easily as a bird flying through the air. Zane walked back down to the alpaca. He enjoyed its company and decided to name it Johnny. He followed Johnny around the forest telling him the stories of all his woes. Zane turned as he heard the crash of metal on rocks. He found himself staring at a tall dark-skinned man with dreadlocks wound tightly together into a bun on top of his head.

"Oh great spirit of the alpacas, I am honored to grace your presence." The man dropped to his knees and prostrated himself to the ground honoring Zane.

"Wait, you can see me?" Zane asked excitedly

"Yes, great one. I am sorry if I offended thee with my eyes. I will never look upon you again," he said in a reverent tone.

"Wait, no, please, I'm no deity. I came here looking for my friends. I actually need your help delivering a message to them," Zane said. The man slowly looked up then ducked his head back to the ground.

"Anything you require, I am your servant."

"Listen, I don't want a servant," Zane said, walking over to pick the man up off the ground. Once again Zane's hands missed the man and moved right through his shoulders.

"Could you stand up?" Zane asked. The man did so and pulled himself up, so he was looking eye-to-eye with him.

"Listen..." Zane didn't know his name and the man was kind enough to fill in the information. "Servant Reggie, sir," he said with a slight bow.

"Reggie, I am not a ghost. I am like you. Just trapped in a different dimension by an evil lady. That's all. I just really need to talk to my friends, Zack and Gliss." The man looked at Zane for a moment then he arched his back and let out the loudest yodel that Zane had ever heard. Tree limbs shook and birds took off, frightened by the sudden blast of noise.

"I have called them back to the yurt as you commanded. Would you grace my home with your presence while we wait for their return?" Reggie asked.

Zane face-palmed but agreed to the offer. He said goodbye to Johnny as they walked back to the large yurt that Zane had spotted earlier. Once inside, Reggie set to work boiling tea. He set out a dish of delicious looking pastries that made Zane's stomach growl. Tea was poured and pastries presented to him. Zane smiled but didn't want to be disappointed because he couldn't eat them. So, they sat tempting him, until Reggie ushered him to eat and drink. Zane sighed then leaned forward out of his bean-bag chair, stretched his hand out and for the second time that day, Zane physically interacted with something from the other dimension. Reggie must have seen the look of surprise on Zane's face because he offered an explanation.

"The secret is alpaca milk. Alpacas exist in two realms at the same time; the physical realm and the spiritual realm, where you currently reside. It has been my power to see beings from both realms. Alpacas are the only animal to be able to do this, so anything made of alpaca wool or milk can be used in either realm." Zane had no idea what Reggie was saying but he was sure enjoying the tasty treats. Zane dropped a pastry as the yurt flap flew inwards and smacked it from his hand. Zack burst in with a dangerous look in his eye and Gliss rolled in next to him looking equally threatening.

"You called, Reggie. Where is the threat?" Zack said, circling the room.

"You misheard my call. The call for danger has a slightly higher intonation at the end. I called an emergency meeting. There is someone here who wishes to speak to both of you." Zack let his hands drop and Gliss stood up straight.

"Who is here?" Gliss asked, scouring the room.

"The Great Spirit of the Alpacas wishes to address you both," Reggie gestured to where Zane sat in the bean bag chair.

"I don't have time for this," Gliss said heading for the door. Zane panicked. He did the only thing he could;

he picked up a pastry and threw it at her. The sugary pastry hit Gliss square in the back. She stopped cold in her tracks.

"Which one of you threw that?" Gliss asked threateningly.

"You have angered the spirit, please, you must let him talk with you," Reggie said, backing away from Zane, who picked up another pastry and held it in his hand. Gliss gawked at the floating pastry. Zane tossed it up and down in his hand, then he sat back down, picked up his cup and began to sip the creamy tea. Gliss hung in the doorway, her jaw agape, watching the impossible. Zack bowed to Zane which made him feel awkward, then Zane gestured for them to sit down and join them. Reggie relayed the invitation and this time both Zack and Gliss took a seat. Zane stood up then took a seat next to Gliss. He remembered what Reggie had said about alpaca-made objects, so Zane stood back up and found two blankets. He wrapped one around his figure then wrapped the second around Gliss, who didn't dare move. Zane pulled her into a hug and this time it worked. His fingers caught her frame and pulled her in close. Gliss sat rigid, so Zane released her and told Reggie to inform them it was Zane.

"The great spirit wants you to know that his name is Zane," Reggie said. Gliss turned to him looking at his form wrapped in blankets.

"Zane, is that really you?" Gliss asked, hope returning to her face.

"Yes," Zane replied, and Reggie interpreted for him.

"I want to believe it is you but how will I be sure it's you. Reggie, can you see him?" Gliss asked.

"Yes, I can see all spirits."

"Great, can you describe in great detail what the great spirit looks like."

"Spirits take on many different faces, but I will do my best. He is a boy who looks to be roughly seventeen, maybe older. He has a singular hair on his chin, that could just be an alpaca hair though. He has brown eyes, and dark brown hair. His shirt is black, one shoulder looks like it is two inches lower than the other one. He is wearing blue jeans; one of the knees is torn open and he is wearing a pair of red sneakers," Reggie finished. Gliss tackled Zane to the ground, and in doing so popped his shoulder back in its socket. Zane yelped at the sudden pain. Tears filled his eyes, but he was happy to be able to feel it again. Gliss didn't let him go for the rest of the meeting. Zane explained what had happened to him, relayed the condition of the dean and watched as Zack's face dropped as he heard the news. Zane finished up his story and then told Reggie to tell them he would be back later as he was going to go back to the school to investigate the dean's condition. Zack stopped Zane.

"This could work to our advantage. Gliss, we could use Zane to spy on council meetings, to leave notes for your parents. To find the information we need to clear your names. For now, we can lay low, help around the farm. Zane should send everybody from the school here. If what he told us is true, they will all be hungry and cold. We can offer some comfort and stability for them. Reggie, you will have your hands full. Can you be the spirit guide you always told me you wanted to be?" Zack asked.

"I will do it, if the Great Alpaca Spirit commands it."

"Then, Reggie, I command you to look after all the spirits who enter here."

Reggie bowed to Zane and Zack dismissed Zane. Zane felt like he had a purpose once again as he flew back to the school. They were going to find a way to get out of this mess one way or another. Zane smiled as he felt a glimmer of hope begin to burn within his chest.

Chapter 16

Persistent Persuasion

Ethan looked down at his shoes as he stood on the front porch of Ruby's house. This was the third time he had tried to talk with her since they had been suspended. The first two attempts had not been in person as he had reached out over social media. Ethan kept wondering why he had promised to help his teachers, even if Ms Dunlap was beautiful. He knew that was not the real reason behind his promise. Ethan could not bring himself to deny what he had seen. He had seen quite a bit more than he had told Gliss. After leaving Ms Dunlap in the hallway fighting Mrs McCoy, Ethan had found himself wandering in darkness peeking through at the little portals of light that spilled through from the mirror dimension.

He had watched as a tall man dressed in black smashed the dean in the face with some kind of glowing black staff. The dean had frozen in place and the lights that had been in front of Ethan had shattered and disappeared into darkness. The lights reappeared and the dean had vanished. Ethan searched the school for someone else to help his class but had, unfortunately, found the rest of the school empty. Ethan shook his head coming out of his daydream and pressed the doorbell for the second time. He waited and listened to the tune that played within the house. The music faded and, just as he was about to leave the house, the door cracked open. Ruby glared at him, her blue eyes like glowing sapphires.

"What do you want, Ethan?" she hissed.

"I just want to talk, like old times, Ruby."

"Too bad you lost the right to talk to me after you left me at prom last year."

She began to close the door, and Ethan rushed forward. He distracted Ruby by pressing his face in the gap and with his other hand he slid a pocket mirror into the home.

"Wait, I told you I wasn't ready for a steady relationship yet."

"Are you ready for one now?" Ruby asked, glaring at him.

"Maybe," he replied through the gap that was continually getting smaller and smaller.

"It's either 'yes' or 'no'. When you decide what you want, then you can come talk to me."

The door closed and Ethan dropped a second-hand mirror on the ground beside him. A moment later he was standing next to Ruby inside the foyer. He flashed a smile at her, and she sighed, then bade him to follow her.

"I have Evelyn here as well. We were just talking about yesterday. I hope you don't mind."

Ethan didn't mind; he found it easy to talk with Evelyn, who was soft spoken. She and Ruby were cousins. They shared the same pair of dazzling blue eyes, and both had blonde hair. Evelyn's hair was a shade lighter and her face slightly more rounded. Other than that, she was very similar to Ruby. They even had powers that worked together. Evelyn came racing down the hallway to them and Ruby shifted the color beneath her to blue. Evelyn stopped in her place then began to pull her feet up with a great deal of effort.

"Let me take him. Let me get a couple good punches in!" she yelled at Ruby.

"No, cuz we have come to terms with how he treated me last year. Ethan, is here to talk, not fight."

"Don't listen to him. He is a liar. Just one punch, please," Evelyn begged, as she continued to crawl like a spider on the wall towards them.

Ruby turned to Ethan,

"Can she punch you just once? It would help her feel like she avenged me."

Ethan considered then agreed to the terms.

"Great, Ev, remember, only one punch as he agreed and that is brave of him to do."

Ruby changed the color back to white. Evelyn glided on the floor as she came up to Ethan, then delivered a solid punch to his stomach, and a kick to his shin. An elbow came and glanced off his chin, knocking him backwards. Then the onslaught stopped.

"I said one punch," Ruby said, helping Ethan from the floor.

"I know, one punch is all he got. He also received, one kick, and one elbow," Evelyn said, folding her arms defiantly across her chest.

"It's good to see you too, Ev," Ethan said, rubbing his chin.

"Go get some ice for his chin," Ruby said with a wave. The ground turned green, and Evelyn ran off, speeding down the corridor faster than should be humanly possible. Ruby helped Ethan down the hallway and to the large table. He sat down and a second later ice was being applied to his face.

"What is it you want to talk about?" Ruby asked, kicking her feet up on the table. Her fingernails began to change to different colors, mainly shades of red, purple, and orange. This allowed Ethan to read her mood. The expression 'wearing your feelings on your sleeve', in Ruby's case should be changed to 'wearing your feelings on your fingers'.

"I came to talk about yesterday."

"You mean, how you stood by and defended our lying, evil teachers?" she said, her fingernails shifting to a deep red. Ethan squirmed in his seat feeling the animosity radiating from Ruby.

"They are not evil. I don't think they planned this any more than we decided to get up in the morning. I didn't tell anyone about what I saw when I left, mainly because I was scared. I didn't know what to trust; my brain or the overwhelming evidence piled against our teachers." Ruby scoffed but her nails shifted to a purple, which meant curiosity. Evelyn didn't say anything, so Ethan continued.

"Haven't you wondered what happened to the rest of the students in our building? Or what happened to the other teachers, even the dean?"

"They all evacuated then went home like the rest of us," Ruby said, swirling a finger on the table slowly painting a picture of a flower on the black surface.

"That's the thing, they didn't. I've been monitoring all online activity for the students in our class, and no one has posted a single thing, no new pictures. It's like they just vanished. Everyone else who was in our class, even most of the other students in the other buildings posted something about yesterday's events. No one from our building did, except for us." Ruby pulled out her cell phone and so did Evelyn, together they began to sift through their feeds visiting students and faculty that were in their building. After ten or so minutes of this the girls set their phones aside.

"So what? It's not like they could just disappear. I think you're overthinking this, but I am curious about what you saw when you abandoned me to die yesterday."

Ethan fought the urge to pull out his hair. He told them what he saw, not leaving out a single detail.

"So, you're telling me that you saw a wizard hit the dean, then everyone disappeared. You also saw Mrs

McCoy fighting with Ms Dunlap? It sounds like, I don't know… a little made up."

"I promise what I saw is the truth."

"I believe you. Gliss was so nice to me last year in advanced clothing design and Mrs McCoy always gave me the creeps," Evelyn said

"Let's say that everything you're telling me is true, even if it is, and our teachers are innocent, how are we going to prove any of it? That is, if we don't get found out ourselves and disappear like the rest of the students. What are you asking us to do?" Ruby said, looking directly into Ethan's eyes.

Her nails shifted to white as he glanced down at them.

"We enrolled in the hero course. I don't know about the rest of you, but I enrolled so that I could make a difference in the world; to learn how to fight against the evils that oppress us. With or without your help, I'm going to try to help our school," he said proudly. Ruby sighed then relaxed. Her fingernails once again shifting colors.

"I'm in," Evelyn said.

Ethan tried not to smile at his success.

"Fine. Fine. I will join in as I too want to be a hero. So where should we start, Mirrious?" she asked.

"For starters, we could try to recruit the rest of the class."

Ruby let out an exasperated laugh.

"Handcuff me now or feed me to a shark because that is what you will get if you try to convince Henry.

The Landreaux family are like dealing with the mafia. You can't just go in and tell them they are wrong. That's how people disappear. Look what he did to your dad," Ruby stated.

"You can't tell me that you are afraid of some punk kid. Besides, my Dad is doing better than ever."

"I have a better solution; why don't you go and talk with Henry and his gang. Ev and I will go talk with Simon and James, if he hasn't been recruited by Henry already."

Ethan did not want to go alone to Henry's; there was a reason that Ruby had been the first person he reached out to.

"Strength in numbers, right? We could just go get Simon and James first. Then, we can all go together to talk with Henry," Ethan offered.

Ruby grinned as she knew that Ethan was scared of Henry just as much as she was.

"Okay, first thing in the morning then?" Ruby asked.

"Sure… thanks again for letting me in and thanks for believing in me," Ethan said. He stood up and walked towards the front door. Ruby caught up to him.

"Listen, I will do this under one condition; you have to agree to be my boyfriend or else we back out. Even if you think you're not ready for the relationship, I will show you that you are. It's not really any different than being friends, we just get to hold hands," Ruby said quietly. Ethan knew that earning her trust and her addition to the team would come at great cost; it always did with Ruby. Ethan turned the knob on the front door and pulled it open.

"I guess I can do this alone," he said, pulling the door closed behind him. A foot stopped the door.

"Fine, just go out on a couple dates with me and come hang out more often. You don't have to be my boyfriend. Even if all we do is remain friends. I just miss talking with you and seeing you," Ruby said

"I can do that. Just a couple of dates though, not like six or seven. Three maximum," Ethan shot back.

"Deal."

The foot moved and the door closed. *What did I just get myself into?* he thought as he began the long walk home. He could have taken a cab but decided that he needed the walk to mull over all that Ruby had said in their conversation. How were they supposed to accomplish anything? They are only a group of want-to-be heroes in school. Just a few kids.

Chapter 17

Secrets

Zane landed softly on the not-grass; he didn't really know what to call it. He had an eerie sensation as he walked through it. He bent down and ran his fingers through the blades. He could feel the slight impression that something was running through his fingers but, as he watched the blades, each passed through his hand one at a time. The phenomenon began to make Zane wonder how he was standing on the ground. If he passed through things like grass, doors, walls and other objects, why was it that he found solid ground beneath his feet? Zane didn't even bother reaching for the door handle, yellow caution tape barricaded the entrance to the school. Zane passed through the door and was surprised to find that he could see the inner workings of the door; every wire that ran through the frame to the locking mechanism set off to the side, down to every last nut and bolt holding the door together.

The lights were all off in the hallway and Zane remembered how he had just up and left Mr Thorne alone. Zane knew that the little man was already fidgety to begin with. Left unattended in the school, unable to interact with his surroundings, Zane wouldn't be surprised to find his teacher huddled in a corner muttering to himself. A few years back Mr Thorne had some kind of episode that nearly landed him in a psychiatric ward in the city. It had come as a shock to Zane. but, after finding out about the incident, he had never really known how to talk to Mr Thorne again. Zane continued down the hallway heading in the direction of the gymnasium. He didn't get far before he found himself being tackled to the ground by another student.

Zane rolled to the side, his weeks of training kicking in and left a small girl that Zane recognized sprawled on the ground to his side.

"Hey! What's the big idea?" Zane asked, rubbing his hip.

"Set me free, you demon!" she yelled back at him with a roar. Zane didn't feel like fighting so he fell backwards and lazily drifted to the ceiling where he watched in amazement as the girl struggled to jump up and grab him.

"Listen... I am not the person who locked us in here. I am a teacher here at the school. Why don't you tell me your name and we can figure out where the rest of your classmates are," Zane offered.

"Lies! We all saw what you did! You are the reason we are all trapped in here! We saw what you and Ms Dunlap did to that class, and now we are all stuck here!" she yelled back. Zane frowned. He hadn't given much thought that he would be seen as an enemy in this realm too. He sighed and continued to fly down the hallway. His pursuer began to say some very unpleasant things, some of which Zane had only heard grown-ups say. Zane flew a little quicker and left the girl behind. He located the gymnasium easily enough. He passed through the doorway and found himself being restrained by many pairs of hands. Zane struggled but it was no use, so he succumbed to the overwhelming force and let them bind his wrists using thread. He watched as some of the faculty began to frantically wrap his wrists over and over with the string as if they were trying to outpace his escape attempt. Zane almost laughed at the ridiculousness of his situation. Now that he knew the truth about alpacas he assumed the frail string was woven with some of their fur.

Once they were satisfied they had subdued the enemy, Zane was hauled to his feet then guided over to an individual dressed in a black cloak. Zane didn't like the look of the individual who seemed to dominate the room with their very presence. He began to wonder who the person was. When they turned, Zane found himself face to face with Mr Thorne! He shuffled awkwardly then began to fidget with his spectacles.

"Ahem!" Mrs Johnson grunted, trying to encourage their leader to engage in conversation with Zane.

"Quiet, Danney, I am trying to think about what to say." He said straightforwardly, the grip on Zane's arm softened then faded away and Zane was left alone standing in silence. Zane became bored of standing and watching Mr Thorne mumble to himself all the while biting fingernails that were already too short. So, he turned and fell forward then took a flight around the room. Groups of students were clumped together. Zane counted roughly thirty students and was relieved to find the girl who had chased him earlier sitting next to a group of girls her age talking. Mr Thorne didn't even notice that Zane had disappeared, so he hovered over to the other teachers who sat on the ground talking amongst themselves. Zane took a seat next to Mrs Johnson. She looked at him with an icy glare, but she didn't move to walk him back up to Mr Thorne.

"So, what are you all talking about?" All conversations ended and every eye fixed on Zane who sat still tied up with string wrapped loosely around his wrists.

"Nothing that concerns you," Mr Farland said in a matter-of-fact kind of way.

"Oh… Okay, well, if you want to know where to find food, or learn about how we all ended up here, or really any pertinent information regarding this place that we are in now, feel free to give me a call."

Zane smiled and found himself gloating inside about the fast and awesome come-back. He stood up and began to walk away when a hand planted itself firmly on his shoulder.

"Wait, don't go. If you really have information that could help us get out of this place then we will listen to you." Zane found Mr Farland standing behind him, his face was full of shame.

Zane immediately felt like a bully. He probably shouldn't have tried to provoke his fellow co-workers. Zane sat back down and began explaining,

"Well, just to correct you, I actually don't have any knowledge on how to escape this place, but I do have information that might help us stay alive until we can find a way out of here."

Zane stopped and saw faces that had been full of hope moments before, dropping into far less appreciative ones. Zane explained about the alpacas and Reggie who could see them, he told them of how he and Gliss had been framed and how Mrs McCoy was the one to blame for this mess. They all listened to his story then understanding dawned on the face of Mrs Johnson.

"That is why we could only pick up this string." She held up the spool of dark thread they had used earlier on Zane.

"If you're telling us the truth then why did our clothes come with us? They aren't made with alpaca fleece. Just to correct everyone, it is fleece or fiber, not fur or hair." Zane recognized the teacher who spoke. She was tall and lanky with burnished auburn-colored hair and olive-green eyes. Zane thought her name was Mrs Randy or something close.

"Well, Mrs…" Zane paused, then trusted his memory. "Randy?"

"It's 'Rondy' not 'Randy'," she said, correcting Zane, who stared back at her before continuing.

"Mrs Rondy, I am going to answer your question with another question. Why can we climb stairs or stand on the ground but have every plant, door or practically any other substance pass through us with little to no effort? Why was I able to smash into the pillar yesterday but I'm able to walk through the door? The answer is: I don't know. I don't understand this place, but there are just a couple things that I can understand, and one of them being anything made with alpaca fleece or milk we can consume and touch. Let's get these kids out of here and to a place where they can have shelter and food. I can only take one at a time. On foot, it would take two or three days to get there. Can anyone else fly?" Zane responded. Mrs Rondy glowered at him but held her tongue. Everyone shook their heads as Zane looked around at the students.

"Can any of your students fly?" Zane asked again, all heads shook. Zane sat down hard and began to rack his brain for an idea. It came to him as he looked out the window. A city bus drove past, and he instantly knew that would be the way to transport everyone from here to the alpaca ranch.

"I've got it. I will be right back. I have to test something," Zane said, before jumping up and breaking his restraints. Mr Thorne finally snapped out of his funk and began to march towards Zane. Zane didn't give him a second thought before heading out the door, and back into the outside world. Zane flew outside. He set out searching for a bus stop and found a bus coming up to a stop full of pedestrians. Zane landed beside everyone, and the bus rumbled up then tooted its horn informing its riders of its arrival.

Zane stepped forward following the line of people. Zane stepped up onto the bus and felt a pang of success at doing so. Feeling confident as the bus began to move, Zane tried to take a seat but fell through the seat and, to his horror, slipped through the bottom of the bus. Zane yelled as he watched a set of big black tires rush towards him. He curled himself up preparing for the pain that would follow. Zane opened his eyes and found the bus rolling down the street away from his position on the ground. He picked himself up then came up with a better idea, Zane flew over to the school sanctioned buses parked out front the other buildings. Zane watched and memorized the code to operate the bus as a driver entered in his code and walked inside to grab his lunch. Zane memorized all the different bus codes and their corresponding numbers. He waited until the school bell chimed and students filed out and boarded the buses. He crossed off the buses that were being filled, then found the one that was used for the general studies building. The bus was empty, and it was the only bus that Zane had not gotten a code for. He sighed then decided to take a look around the inside for clues to find the code.

Zane stopped short as he met the face of the bus driver sitting in his chair looking sad. The man looked over at him then jumped back in surprise.

"Are you like me?" Zane nodded.

"Kid. you would be better off walking home. not like the kids yesterday didn't try that. The kids yesterday tried to but most of them returned to the school with bleary eyes and runny noses. I just wish I could still drive." The man returned to trying to grab the steering wheel as if he would be able to do it eventually.

"Do you want to help me get these kids to a safe place?" Zane asked him. The driver looked up.

"How? If I can't even drive?"

Zane smiled and told the man to wait there for a few more hours. As Zane flew away, he suspected he didn't have to tell the driver to stay there. Zane could have left him for a week, and he was sure that the man would still be attempting to do the same thing. Zane found the alpaca ranch and quickly located Reggie, who directed him towards a pile of old clothes, including hand woven moccasins. Zane then stuffed as many alpaca blankets in a large duffle bag as he could, then set back off towards the school. Zane was pleased with his work and, judging by the look on the school bus driver's face, he was too. Every inch of the bus was coated in alpaca fleece blankets, pillowcases, coats, socks, and about every other item of clothing one could think of. Bill, the driver, did not quite fit in the moccasins that Zane had brought for him. Zane and Bill struggled for a couple of minutes until the moccasins were covering at least the top three inches of Bill's foot.

Mr Thorne stepped out through the front door of the school. He did not look happy,

"Mr Whitlock, I am not sure how you escaped your restraints, but this time you'll be locked up for your crimes against the school and its students."

Mr Thorne flinched at every noise that rattled through the air. Zane could tell the man was not handling the situation well, so Zane ran at him, taking into account his skittishness. Zane reached him quickly then stood with his nose only inches away from Mr Thorne.

"Lance, I suggest that you listen to me. I am going to save our students. Whether you're part of the picture or not is entirely up to you," Zane hissed, finally remembering his teacher's first name. The confrontation was enough. What vigor the man had left, vanished and he conceded. Zane stepped away from him and entered the school building. With the help of the other teachers, all the students were accounted for and loaded onto the school bus. The ride wasn't as long as Zane had thought it would be, but he had caught glimpses of other people looking in at their driver who seemed to have no head or a left arm. What was visible was wrapped loosely in a large shaggy looking shawl. The last mile of the journey, they ended up losing two boys who flew off their seats after the bus hit a particularly large pothole. Zane had been sent back once someone noticed they had slipped out. Zane finished carrying the last boy back into the ranch. Zane found Gliss who was staring in confusion at the mass of floating blankets, and different articles of alpaca clothing.

He walked over to her and placed a blanket over her shoulders and wrapped the other end over his head. She flinched then realized that no one else would have the guts to do it. Zane welcomed the warm embrace and even found himself liking the punch that came after. He delivered a soft punch of his own. She smiled then began to ask him questions about how it had gone. Zane tried to answer and Gliss stopped, then face palmed realizing that she couldn't actually speak with him. Zane picked up a stick and began to draw in the dirt. She stopped and began to read the words he had written. 'Good, I had some trouble with Mr Thorne but, other than that, everything went well.'

"Good, hey, Zack wants you to take him to his uncle. Wait here then show him where you are."

She left before Zane had a chance to write another message. She returned and Zack followed in tow. "You ready to show me where my uncle is?" Zack asked.

Zane wrote the word 'yes' in the soft dirt. Zack looked down then offered a pair of gloves, and a cell phone to Zane. He pulled the gloves on and stashed the phone in the bag he had borrowed earlier. Together they set out. Zack beat Zane to the school and Zane found his friend waiting just outside the caution tape that had been placed around the building. Zane landed next to him. Zack waited for Zane to open the door from the inside. It was harder than he had anticipated; the gloves, backpack and phone didn't pass through the door like he could. Zane had to find an open window to be able to open the door for Zack.

Together they walked in silence. Zane led the way down the dark corridors, Zack followed. When Zane rounded the final corner he froze and held up a hand for Zack to stop.

Jane McCoy sat talking with the frozen statue of the dean. Zack tried to press forward but Zane firmly planted a hand on his shoulder barring his pathway forward. Zane retreated down the hallway then pulled out his phone, typing out a message explaining to Zack what he had seen. Zack's face began to turn red, and he marched past Zane. This time there would be no stopping Zack. He rounded the corner and Zane peered around the corner to watch the exchange. Zane watched as Jane turned her head, looked at Zack, smiled, then Zane watched as she melted into the other dimension. Zack stopped short. He popped his knuckles and pushed his hair back out of his face.

"Listen, lady. I know that you trapped my uncle and the rest of the school. Let them go and I might spare you," Zack yelled at her.

"Really, what are you going to do, shake your fist at me?" she said, trying to imply how useless Zack's power was.

"I warned you!" Zack yelled running forward. The ground began to shake all around Zane, who watched as something changed around him. It was as if the air was becoming thick. Zane felt slightly nauseous. There was something familiar about the sensation, but it was over in a flash, as Zack joined Zane in the dimension. Jane had simply pushed Zack and he had fallen into the sub-dimension. Zack stood and looked at his belongings.

"I was actually hoping you would show up sometime. Just trying to tie up some loose ends. Now, tell me where Ms Dunlap is, and I will let you live." Jane threatened.

"I don't know where she is now... if you asked me a couple hours ago, I could have told you. She is probably somewhere far from here," Zack lied.

"You don't think I'm serious. I won't hesitate to kill you."

"Really! I don't know. The last place we were together was my buddy's place in the city. His name is Reggie," Zack said frantically, trying to make it look like the sincere truth.

"Does Reggie have a last name?"

"Dominguez. He lives on seventh avenue and Heating. Apartment two zero two."

"Thanks for being a dear, but don't think about going anywhere, I will track you down. I will know real soon if you are lying. Just hold tight. Oh, and Zane, you can come out of hiding. I will fulfill my promise real soon."

With that she oozed into the other dimension. Zane gave a wide berth to Jane as she passed. Even though he knew that he was invisible to her, he didn't want to chance it. Once she was gone, Zack walked over to Zane and bummed a glove from him. He walked over to where his phone had dropped and bent over to pick it up.

"Zack, what are you doing? How are we supposed to warn Gliss? Also, she is going to be back to kill us both as soon as she finds out you lied to her."

"Bro, I kinda was curious how it felt to be a ghost, but I also wasn't thinking when I rushed here," he said, looking around until his eyes fell on his frozen uncle. Zack walked forward and rested a hand on the life-like statue. Zane walked up and joined him. Zack froze and closed his eyes.

"What is it?" Zane asked him.

"Shh! I'm trying to feel."

Zane didn't press any further, instead he waited. The floor beneath him began to vibrate like it had earlier. Zane watched as his friend concentrated. The vibrations increased, then Zack became a statue just like his uncle. Zane reeled back and fell hard on the floor,. He looked at his hands, trying to inspect them for the same statue-like disease that had overcome his friend. Seeing that everything was fine, Zane rushed back up and put his hand on Zack and tried to pry him from the dean. "Zack... No... No, not you, too. This was going to be hard enough with just the three of us. What am I going to do now?" Zane shouted at Zack, who stayed true to his new form and stood unmoving.

Zane felt the anger rising within himself and let his fist fly into the statues. Punch after punch landed. Zane stopped, breathing hard. He looked at the dean and noticed the dean's face had contorted and was moving as slow as molasses. Zane recognized the face as pain, and he immediately began to apologize for punching the man.

Zane watched in awe as the statues began to move while the ground began to hum. The pitch began to climb to an uncomfortable level, until it leveled out, sounding like a train whistling straight in his ear. Zane slammed his hands over his ears trying to block out the sound. His head began to swim, and Zane felt his body hit the ground. The pain didn't even register as he lay helpless on the floor. For a second he thought he saw a bright flash of light, then Zane's vision faded to black.

Chapter 18

The Pact

Ethan felt like puking. After the road they had just been on, it was hard for anyone to be feeling great. Well, everyone except Henry, who looked as if he were enjoying every little jostle and bump. The music that blasted all around Ethan made him feel like he was on a bushwhacking adventure, hiking through the thick foliage of a jungle. Ruby sat across from him with her arms folded. She looked like she was too upset to be feeling much of anything. Evelyn had her hand over her mouth as the vehicle swayed back and forth. Logan, who sat next to her, tried to keep as much distance from her as possible, with the ever-present threat of already eaten lunch coming back up seeming inevitable. Calvin sat wearing his thick black glasses and his hair slicked back. Simon sat directly to Ethan's left. He took up more space than Ethan had originally imagined was possible but, each time Ethan tried to fight him for more space on the bench seat, it was impossible to even move a single hair that stuck out on his legs. They felt like needles and gave Ethan papercuts each time their knees met.

The muffled voice of James came from behind the cushions. Ethan pushed the middle cushion down and James' face came into view. His dark hair covered the majority of his face.

"How much longer? It's starting to feel a little stuffy in here." Ethan shrugged but Simon leaned over and was all too happy to tell James to just sit back and relax, that it couldn't be more than five minutes away. It was the third time that Ethan had heard the tall Polynesian tell someone that they were only five minutes away. He was beginning to wonder what was with Simon and his obsession with five minutes, when the music took on a dramatic change. The pace quickened and the drums began to thunder. The engine revved and the vehicle lurched sideways. Ethan searched for a handhold, then slid into Simon, who, unlike the rest of the people in the off-road monster of a car, didn't move a centimeter.

It had been easier than Ethan thought to convince Henry to join their cause. All it had taken was Ruby to promise to join the gang. It had taken a little coaxing and the promise of a fourth date to persuade her to join. Henry had informed them, after Ruby had joined, that he sent the video off to be inspected and the video he showed was drastically different from the one they all saw before. A fat man with dark skin and a mass of hair on his head, along with a short plump woman with a green shirt, had been the individuals who had really committed the crime. Henry said the video had been tampered with by a low-level technopath.

Ruby protested that Henry had withheld information from them and said she no longer wanted to join the group. Henry didn't let her back out and told them the deal had been struck and Ruby needed to keep her part of the pact and join the group on their adventure. Henry had also been kind enough to have suits made for everyone except Ethan. Ethan had suspected as much. He had ordered his weeks before as soon as he signed up for the program. His wasn't as high quality as the rest of the group's but he didn't care much for high quality. Ethan also had his suspicion on the legality of how Henry had obtained the suits. Some of the features seemed to be illegal in most countries except Russia. When Ethan pressed Henry, the only answer he supplied had been,

"I know a guy who knows a guy. I could even get you a suit… for the right price."

The more Ethan got to know Henry; the scarier Henry became. He was just glad to sort-of be on Henry's good side. Ethan had blown off the offer of a new suit, figuring the price would likely be too high, then packed his own suit. Once they were all geared up, they had all decided to go back to the school to look for clues as to what had happened to the faculty and their fellow students.

It was RoseAnne who spotted the school bus and phantom driver leaving the school. The van they were riding in performed an illegal U-turn and followed the bus. Once the police had been evaded and the bus located, the pavement ended, and they stopped to watch the bus climb high into the mountains. Henry didn't want to drive his van on the gravel, so they waited for the ridiculous looking off-road vehicle he called and ordered to show up. It was painted bright red with black stripes, the entire car mainly consisted of roll cages, and oversized tires that lifted the car high into the air, giving it an impressive ground clearance. The down-side was it only had eight seats. James volunteered to ride in the trunk.

Instead of following the same road as the bus, Henry had decided to take a more 'creative' way to their destination. This led them to the theme-park thrill-level ride that they were on now. Fortunately, the path leveled out after a steep descent and Ethan found himself breathing easier. He glanced out the window and immediately frowned as he saw the van parked only a couple hundred yards away, they'd been driving for nearly an hour.

"Henry, take a look at where you have managed to get us," Ethan said, speaking up from the back. All eyes turned to look at the silver van.

"Aww, Henry, you drove us in a circle, you dummy!" Calvin yelled up at him, Ethan heard a muffled groan coming from behind him.

"Okay, move over. I'm driving us the rest of the way," Ruby said unbuckling her seat belt. Henry was quickly shoved to the back. Ruby rolled down the window and touched the door of the vehicle to turn it to a bright pink color. Henry started to yell at her but was drowned out when the engine revved faster and louder than anyone had heard before.

"Hey! Take it easy, I don't want a single scratch, you hear me?" The rear wheels lost their traction, and they began to fishtail. Ruby slammed the shifter into second gear, the fishtail ended and they shot up the road. Eight screams sounded as they sped down the small dirt road at an insane speed. Ethan smiled as he saw real fear in the eyes of Henry. The engine was loud enough to drown out the stupid music. Five minutes later they came to an abrupt halt and Ruby announced they were at their destination. She shut the engine off and tossed the keys back to Henry. James rolled out of the trunk and hit the ground hard. A plume of dust shot up around him and he lay groaning for a solid couple of minutes. Ethan nearly threw up but managed to keep it down. Evelyn was not so lucky, neither was Logan; he couldn't get his seat belt off fast enough and was rewarded with a new color of shoes to walk around in. They regrouped once everyone was settled. Ruby walked up alongside Ethan and nuzzled into his arm. He sighed and they walked past the bus only to freeze in place.

"I'm not the only one seeing this, right?" RoseAnne asked.

Everyone shook their heads in response. Floating articles of clothing and hovering blankets walked around the grove in front of them, some of them mingling with and petting the alpacas that seemed to be enjoying the company of ghosts. The hair on Ethan's neck shot up as a scarf approached them. It flailed in the air then went rigid, as if someone was pulling both ends together tight. The scarf then wrapped itself around the unseen hands and a stick was picked up from the ground. Evelyn let out a little screech as the stick began to form letters on the ground.

Welcome, esteemed guests, you will find our leader in the tent conversing with the masters. The stick then drew an arrow that pointed further into the grove, where a large white yurt sat proudly with its flaps open.

"Guys, I don't think we should go in there, what if it's a trap?" Logan said, his face pale, all blood drained from within.

"I'm not scared of anything, you can wait here if you like, but I'm about to get to the bottom of this," Henry said, as proud-sounding music began to play around him.

"Let's send a scout. Ev, go check things out," Ruby said.

The ground in front of them changed to a bright vibrant green. "Why does it have to be me?" she complained.

"Because I said so... also our only other option is sending Henry. I don't trust him to keep quiet."

Henry shot Ruby a look as if her words had wounded him.

"Fine, I will go."

Evelyn setoff at a blinding speed. Gloves, blankets, socks, and other pieces of clothing fell to the ground as she whizzed past. Ethan watched as Ruby followed her every twist and turn, keeping up with her cousin's speed. Evelyn circled the yurt then peeked inside. A second later she stood in front of them.

"She is here… Ms Dunlap… She is talking with a big, weird-smelling fellow."

The report gave them the courage to cross the field of ghosts. Once they reached the yurt, Henry stepped inside, holding his hand out to stop the others.

"Wait!" He paused and everyone waited, "yeah, we're all good. She was telling the truth," Henry said. Evelyn glared at Henry.

The yurt was smaller than Ethan had assumed. The space wasn't small, but it was cluttered with all sorts of chairs made from some kind of mismatched material.

"Guys, how did you find us? You're not here to take me in, right?" Gliss asked, shoving her chair over as she stood up preparing to run.

"No, of course not. We are here to help find the rest of our school. We know that something fishy is going on. It was Ethan who first noticed that no one was posting on their social media accounts. So, we rallied together and saw a mysterious bus driving itself from our school and we followed it all the way here," Ruby explained.

"Yeah, she's right, sorry for attacking you back there. I found the real video. Unless Mr Whitlock is a big fat guy, then you guys are not our perps," Henry apologized "Good to hear. As for the rest of the students from the school, look no further. They're all around you." Gliss gestured to the empty field of ghosts and alpacas.

"I don't understand," Logan said.

"You might want to sit down for this, it's kind of a long story. I can't believe that Ethan didn't tell you what he saw."

"He did say something about an old lady kicking your butt, and a wizard hitting the dean," RoseAnne said, waving her hand dismissively in the air.

"What? A wizard?"

Stories were swapped and more details were given about the wizard and the dean. Soon the group sat digesting the information in silence, except for some light background music. Reggie broke the silence.

"Well, welcome, Friends of the Great Alpaca Spirit." Everyone turned to look at Reggie.

"The spirits are requesting food. Could I solicit some extra help in providing meals for the school? I have been making alpaca milk stew all day." They reluctantly agreed and bowls of soup were soon distributed to every ghostly member of the school. Once dinner was served and bellies were filled, the dishes began to pile up.

Ethan found himself washing dishes alongside Henry. The river babbled and Henry's relaxing music began to flow with the sounds of the burbling water.

"So… anything new?" Henry said, breaking the almost silence.

"Nope"

"How's your dad?"

"Fine, as if you don't already know."

"Listen, just because my Dad didn't give yours the promotion at the store, doesn't mean that we can't be friends,"
Henry said. Ethan stared at him. Anger began to boil in his veins.

"You have no right! You're not the one who watched their dad work so hard, only to be rewarded with nothing. He deserved the promotion to store manager. Don't drag up the past. We can never be friends. You can take your offer and…" Ethan was interrupted as a rock shifted and tumbled down the creek. The source of the disturbance stepped out from behind a tree; a large alpaca continued its path down the stream. Ethan and Henry both turned to watch the graceful animal with its long neck and powerful looking eyes. This particular alpaca wore a collar and, as it approached, Ethan read the collar. The original name, "Timothy Longneck" had been scratched out and the name 'Johnny' had been written with a black sharpie.

"Hello, Johnny, what happened to Timothy Longneck? Did you not like it any more?"
Ethan joked, trying to forget about the conversation he was having with Henry. Henry stepped in closer to examine the name tag, scoffed then stepped back.

"It was probably one of the students, you know the invisible ones, those vandals. Don't worry, Timothy Long Legs, I will get you a new collar that no one will be able to vandalize," he said, reassuring the animal. Johnny wandered off and left the two to continue cleaning. No conversation took bloom, but the dishes became the cleanest they had been in years. Together they returned the large stack of bowls and spoons.

Ethan and Henry made their way over to the others who had gathered around the car. Ethan knew that if he stayed out any later his parents would be wondering where he was. They had all come to the same conclusion and had naturally gathered around the car. Ethan spotted an extra person in the group, and he recognized Gliss leaning up against one of the large tires. Henry shoved Ethan to the side then slicked his hair over to one side before stepping up to Gliss. She had told them all to drop the formalities and just call her by her real name.

She explained that even if her and Zane's names were cleared, there was only a very slight chance that they would be given the opportunity to return to their positions. The gang circled around as Gliss called for them to listen to her.

"Guys, I have some concerning news, I have been waiting for Zack to return with Zane. They set off earlier today to go look at the dean. I'm beginning to worry that something might have happened. I know that most of you have curfews but sometimes you just have to do the right thing no matter the consequences. I need a ride to the school; there is something that I need to see myself."

"Yeah, we will take you anywhere you want to go," Henry said with a smile.

"Wait, don't you remember we had to stuff James in the trunk just to get here; there is no room for another person," Calvin said, discarding a long piece of grass he had been chewing on.

"Don't worry, I can fly down to the edge of the road. I don't know if I should involve you guys, you don't have any training, or suits for that matter. And if you are seen with me, it is very likely that law enforcement will group you in with Zane and me. Maybe I should just go alone," Gliss said the last part more to herself than to the group. Henry smiled, then began to make his way to the trunk, his gang followed behind. Soon suits were being put on. Ethan removed his from the backpack he had brought. Gliss watched them and she smiled, saying, "I knew you guys were put in the hero course for a reason. I am going to suit up too."

Ethan watched as she tore away from the group leaving them all standing looking at each other.

"We look stupid," Ruby said flatly, looking at Henry who stood with blue and green colored speakers popping through his suit.

"I kind of like it. I think we look rad," Logan countered, looking around at the rest of the group.

All eyes fell on Ethan, his cheeks began to burn red with embarrassment. He had well over sixty pocket mirrors strapped to different parts of his body. The suit itself was silver and black. He looked like a walking disco ball he had seen in a history book.

"Well, everyone except Ethan."

"I think he looks very interesting," Ruby said, trying to find some piece of evidence to defend his suit. Ethan knew that 'interesting' isn't necessarily a good thing, it could be bad. Laughter erupted and it didn't last long but it did happen. Gliss returned a little while later, she looked with surprise at the group of shiny new suits. Ruby's continued to change different colors; she looked like some kind of walking chameleon.

"Race you to the road," Gliss said with a smile.

"You're on," Ruby said, snatching the keys right from Henry's hand. Ethan rushed to the vehicle and pulled himself in. Simon moved at his usual lax speed and soon they found themselves sputtering glitter, as it rained down from the sky above. The engine ignited and Ruby took off down the road. More screaming followed for the rest of the ride down to the street far below.

Chapter 19

Brawl

Gliss watched as her former students zipped down the rough road. She smiled fondly at them. She knew that she was asking a lot from students she had only met a handful of times. She felt a warmth bloom inside her chest, like warm sticky honey that clung to her insides. She felt hope rising inside her. She just had to find out what had happened to Zack and Zane. She had been worried since they left earlier in the day.

Gliss watched as the last remaining rays of sunlight caught the glitter as it fell through the sky, spraying dazzling rainbows in hues of green to burnishing flashes of red and orange. She caught her breath as she saw the rare purple as it blended with the remaining deep red of the sunlight on the horizon. For a moment, everything moved in slow motion. Gliss felt the freedom that Zane had always talked about; the yearning to just fly, to no particular destination but to chase the fleeting moment with every ounce of character you have left.

The moment ended. But, the feelings would never be forgotten. Gliss took hold of the feeling and tucked it inside of her heart where it would be protected from the grasps of the outside world. That feeling would be a well-kept treasure only to be felt and shared with a select few. Gliss began her descent and landed softly next to the oversized van. She waited for a while, letting the breeze catch her hair, tossing it freely. The sound of an engine roaring brought Gliss back to reality. She watched as the terrified faces of her students pulled up in the vehicle. They hopped out and Henry ran for the closest bush, while pulling at his helmet. Some of the others laid on the ground groaning. Gliss knew that they would be met with the same problem of the maximum occupants the van could carry. She found herself wishing that she would be allowed to ride with Ruby as it looked like so much fun. Gliss heard a faint pounding coming from the back of the vehicle. She walked around to investigate. It was then she realized that James must still be stuck in the trunk. Gliss lifted the latch and James fell out onto the ground. He moaned and lay with the others. Ruby, however, rounded the car and beamed at Gliss, her helmet tucked off to one side.

"Meet you at the school?" Gliss asked everyone. Henry waved her on and said they would catch up. Gliss smiled, happy she didn't even have to persuade them to let her ride in the awesome-looking vehicle. Ruby ran back to the driver's seat. Gliss didn't mind as she buckled the safety straps and Ruby started the engine. Ruby put her hand down on the steel frame, the car suddenly shifted to a dark violet color, the headlights turned hot pink, they waved their goodbyes and shot off down the road. Gliss laughed as she felt the wind rushing past her, she loved the exhilaration of going so quickly. Ruby was happy that she had found a suitable driving companion. Gliss could tell because the car topped out and the speedometer showed an incredible one-hundred-and-twenty-three. Gliss thought they would slow down once they reached the city and merge in with the regular traffic. Instead Ruby darted in between cars and slid through gaps, narrowly missing street signs and low-hanging tree limbs. Medians did not prove to be an obstacle. When the police sirens and lights began to follow them Ruby changed the color of the vehicle and Gliss's suit to black, so black that when Gliss placed her hand on her leg she couldn't see her gloved fingers. She realized her visor must have been changed to the same color because when she held up her hand in front of her face, she couldn't see it either. Trusting Ruby, Gliss held on and just listened to the sounds of those in pursuit. Soon the only sound that Gliss heard was the shifting of gears and the squealing of brakes. Minutes passed before her vision was restored.

Gliss looked down and was happy to see her suit in its original color. She watched as they skidded to a halt behind the school. Ruby backed in between two large garbage bins. Just as Gliss was going to hop out, Ruby stopped her then jumped out and snapped a picture of the wall behind them.

"Hold still, this is going to be a bit tricky."

Gliss did as Ruby asked and held as still as she could. Ruby pressed her hand on the car and the colors began to shift once more. Gray lines began to form on her suit along with very realistic looking bricks. Gliss realized what was happening as two officers pulled up surveying the area. Gliss held her breath as they pulled out flashlights. The beam of light fell on them and Gliss nearly sneezed, but, luckily, she found she was able to suppress the bodily function. They inched closer and Gliss tried not to move. Crackling came over the receiver and called the police officers back; the voice said they had spotted the vehicle moving southbound a block away. The officers hopped back in their cars and drove off.

The illusion faded and both girls looked at each other with relief.

"Nice camouflage, not to mention your driving skills, that was awesome!" Gliss said excitedly.

"Thanks, I have had some practice."

"I can tell," Gliss said hopping out of the UTV.

"Let's go wait for the others. I'm sure they will be here soon." Gliss said.

"No way! We have time to kill. The way that Henry drives, we will be eating lunch tomorrow, before he gets here," Ruby said, complaining.

"I'm positive they will be here quicker than you think they will be."

Gliss and Ruby began to make their way to the front of the school trying to look as inconspicuous as possible. It wasn't working, as their suits drew the attention of a young boy and his mother walking past the school. The boy pointed and tried to get his mom to look. The young mother took a glance at the two then ushered her son more quickly down the sidewalk. Ruby changed their suits to look like clothing. From a distance, the illusion probably was convincing but up close the bulky suit looked strange as it tried to mimic the natural wrinkles that formed in clothes. Ten minutes later, the van pulled up and the rest of the gang joined them standing in front of the school looking at the caution tape that now plastered the door. Gliss didn't have her keycard any more. But, it didn't matter. She was sure if she did and tried to use it, the building would be surrounded by police in minutes. Vines shot out and filled the cracks that lined the door. Soon they grew in size and the whole door was ripped from the building. Rose carefully directed the vines to place the door down, so it leaned against the building.

Gliss watched as Logan downed a tube of gravel. His loose-fitting suit began to stretch tightly as his muscles grew.

"I don't know what we are looking for but be on the lookout for any suspicious activity. Calvin, can you keep a lookout for any police or threatening looking individuals and warn us if they approach?"

He nodded and took a position behind a bush that sprouted up as RoseAnne waved a hand over the area. Together they entered the school. Gliss noticed the constant theme music that played as if they were all in a movie. She took comfort in the music as the dim emergency lights flickered above. Built-in lights came on from their helmets lighting the hallway before them. Unknowingly, Gliss found herself leading them all to their classroom. As she rounded the corner she noticed a backpack lying on the ground and recognized the bag. It had been the one Zane had taken with him this morning. Gliss found the gloves he had been wearing too. They were in the hallway crumpled next to a garbage bin.

"Zane... Zack," Gliss called out, searching for her friends. The gloves stayed crumpled, and the bag didn't move. She called louder and her students began to follow suit, calling after the two.

An hour elapsed and there was still no sign of either of them. Gliss began to worry that something awful must have happened. The hairs on the back of her neck froze as she heard the oh so familiar sound of high heels clicking on the polished concrete floor.

"Run, get out of here now," Gliss yelled at her students. They looked at her but most of their expressions were concealed by helmets. It took the sound of maniacal laughter coming from beyond the darkness to get them moving. They raced down the hallways. Gliss felt her heart beating inside her chest, and it was unusually fast. She was not one to run from a fight, but for some unknown reason, she found herself running. It took her a minute to identify the reason; she was protecting her students. She knew that if it came down to them all fighting Jane, there would most likely be a few casualties. Gliss had no problem putting her life in danger, but she found it incredibly difficult to willingly endanger her students.

Everyone stopped abruptly and Gliss had to reach out and catch hold of Simon to avoid colliding with the gathered mass. Masked figures dressed in all-black stood blocking their path; some looked big and muscly, others small but vicious.

"Ethan, can you get us all out of here?" Gliss asked.
"Maybe, I have never tried taking someone with me."
"Well now is the time to try," Gliss hissed.

"Everybody, grab on to me and no matter what, don't let go," Ethan said.

No one wasted a second, as all hands grabbed on, and a mirror dropped to the ground.

Gliss found herself walking through a dark hallway with small openings of light shining through. She caught a glimpse of a sink, she looked through another and recognized a row of lockers, Ethan pulled them all along, he picked up the pace as he looked behind him. Gliss looked over her shoulder and found seven dark figures chasing them. A large crevasse formed ahead of them but, as Ethan neared, a bridge appeared. They crossed the bridge and, just as Gliss stepped off it vanished. Ethan kept towing them along and he gasped as the figures jumped over the crevasse. Ethan turned down a second hallway and they crossed a second large crack. Gliss began to breathe hard. They had been running for what felt like over a mile. Ethan pulled them sharply to the right and they began to fall through an opening. Gliss heard a small popping noise and found herself standing in an unfamiliar place.

"Where are we?" Gliss asked.

"Office building, the one next to the bank," Ethan said through gasps.

"Who are those guys, and why are they chasing us?" Evelyn asked.

"No time, we need to move, those guys might not be here on the same floor as us, but they could be close by," Ethan said.

Gliss took the lead and found a stairwell leading down. She began to take the stairs two at a time. She reached the landing just in time for the door to blow off its hinges. Gliss narrowly missed the door, but the chair that came next caught her square in the chest. She flew backwards and crashed into the metal banister. Gliss stood on shaky legs, took aim and fired. She heard a grunt as glitter filled the air. Gliss looked up and grimaced as she saw they were on the first floor; This would be their only way out.

"We are going to have to fight our way out," Gliss said.

Ethan and Henry walked over and helped Gliss stand. Her vision was finally beginning to settle. She shook her head and assured them she was fine.

"You heard her, let's show these goons who they are up against," Henry yelled, his music becoming intense.

Simon walked ahead of everyone insisting they stay behind him. They walked single file searching for the attacker who was in the room. Glitter settled and they saw the line of desks that had been blasted back from the attacker. A fireball took Simon in the chest, the flames spread around him. It was followed by a second and third. Next, a desk flew through the air to Gliss's right. Logan stepped in front of it, easily deflecting the office supply. A balloon appeared in front of Gliss, and it popped, but it sounded wrong. Gliss felt herself being pulled towards the spot where the balloon had exploded. Gliss tried to pull away, but the harder she tried, the faster her body was pulled forward. She collided with Ruby who stood in front of her. They fell to the ground. Ruby frowned and slapped her palm down on the ground. The entire ground shifted to red. Evelyn ran off heading towards a large man who was trying to remove a large load-bearing steel pillar that extended up through the ceiling. Gliss watched as she punched him, the man flew backwards smashing through a glass door. Gliss pulled herself up, just in time to hear Jane McCoy's too familiar voice,

"Glissandra, when will you realize that you have been beaten? When I found Zack earlier snooping around, it didn't take me long to dispatch him and your boyfriend. I have to admit it was hard to watch them die. Struggling, and gasping for air. I tried to show mercy by making it quick."

"Shut up, you're lying, you monster!" Gliss yelled back, searching for Jane. Gliss stepped out from the others and ran towards the darkest corner of the room. She smiled as she saw the surprise on Jane's face. Gliss landed a punch on her jaw. Jane stumbled back and Gliss lashed out with a kick driving it deeply into her ribs. Jane smiled, grabbed her leg and pulled Gliss to the floor. A weird feeling passed over Gliss and she held her breath trying not to puke. She noticed Jane running away. Gliss ran after her. Jane began to melt, leaving Gliss in the sub dimension. Gliss gritted her teeth and used her jet-pack at full power. She exploded forward like a rocket and slammed into Jane just as her shoulders were melting into the floor.

They shot out of the dimension and up towards the ceiling. They struck each other and Gliss held Jane pinned against the ceiling keeping the glitter jets going. From above, she looked around at the chaos. Piles of mushrooms and compost lay all around the room. Vines, trees and bushes littered the ground, some of which were on fire. Logan lay unmoving on the floor. Henry was helping Ruby out of the front doors. Three of the guys dressed in black also lay unconscious. RoseAnne was fighting a man with a wizard's staff. Just as he swung his staff at her Evelyn ran up from behind and struck him on the head with a stapler. The man yelped and fell to the floor. Gliss watched as three of the pillars gave out, the ceiling shuddered, and the building began to squeak.

"Get everyone out now! Even the bad guys, we all need to leave. The building is going down!" Gliss screamed. Jane laughed and kicked Gliss away. She fell to the floor and took aim as Jane fell. Gliss fired every sphere she had in her inventory. Glitter began to fill the air. It became so thick that even Gliss began to panic, turning around as she watched Jane and two other villains run up the stairwell.

"You're not getting away that fast." Gliss yelled as she ran out the door and out onto the landing.

"Wait!" She heard Ethan yell from behind her. Gliss waited for a moment, Ethan burst onto the landing and together they ran up the stairs in pursuit of the villains. Eventually they reached the top and followed Jane out onto the top of the building.

"Just two of you? How pathetic!" Jane sneered.

"You're going down, you and your evil gang!" Gliss yelled back.

"Honey, I love your enthusiasm. True, we won't win the day, but we got what we came for. Have fun until we meet again. Oh, and sorry about your boyfriend," Jane said.

Gliss took aim, then remembered she had used all her spheres. She would just have to stall until her body could produce more. She glared at the interface on her arm willing the number to go up.

"We're not done here, Jane. You can be a coward and run after I kick your butt," Jane froze.

"Glissandra, you…"

Jane was cut off as a sphere caught her in the shoulder. Gliss stood, shocked. She hadn't fired any spheres. She checked the display, but it showed three spheres.

"No one, I mean no one, can call my niece Glissandra. That is reserved for family members only" a voice called out.

The sphere did not explode with glitter; instead it hissed out a spray that caught Jane by surprise and made her cough fiercely. Gliss turned to see her Aunt Margery standing behind her in a shimmering orange suit. Jane recovered but Margery fired a second sphere. Jane was ready this time and the sphere melted only to catch Ethan right in the face. The sphere broke and the spray went directly into his eyes.

Ethan yelled and fell to his knees. Margery ran at Jane, and tackled her to the ground. Gliss fired two spheres at the remaining goons. She recognized one of them as he twirled a staff, trying to bat the sphere away. It didn't work, as glitter exploded around him, and the staff flew from his hands falling over the side of the building. The man yelled and watched as his staff fell towards the ground below. The glitter cleared. Gliss found that everyone who had been standing there except Ethan and herself had vanished.

"Come on, we have to get out of here," Gliss said pulling at Ethan's hand. As they headed towards the door, the building lurched and sent them tumbling to the ground. Ethan rolled away and blindly caught hold of a pole that jutted out from the roof. Gliss screamed and she watched one of her boots fly off the edge of the falling building caught on an old refrigerator unit. Their fastest escape had been cut off. Gliss felt dread filling her. They weren't going to make it.

Chapter 20

Rescue

Zane gained consciousness and he watched as the floor below him rocked back and forth. His head felt like it was filled with cotton. He shook it slightly as he heard muffled voices. They sounded like they were speaking a different language. Zane tried to turn to look up at the person who was carrying him, but he was unable to twist far enough to see anything besides a wrinkled blue shirt. Zane waited a while longer until he was able to make out the words,

"Don't know why we get the boring jobs. You would think that they would value their employees, I mean, shoot, I've been with the corporation for nearly two years now."

"Right, I know I've been doing body clean-up forever," a second voice said from Zane's right. Zane decided to act like he was still unconscious, while he listened.

"Earl, how do you think this kid got involved with..."

Zane didn't catch the name as the second man let out a whirling sneeze. Some of the spray landed on

Zane's face as they continued to walk. He tried and was able to suppress a sound of disgust. Zane really wanted to know the name of the organization Mrs McCoy worked for. He knew the information would be a huge lead.

"I don't know, maybe drugs or something, well. Let's drop this body off at the incinerator, then grab a bite to eat."

"Sounds good to me."

Incinerator! Zane did not like the idea of becoming BBQ. He decided it was time to escape. Slamming his chin into the man's back, Zane was able to break the man's grip. He fell towards the floor then took off down the hallway. Zane turned around to see two men dressed in black robes. Earl must be the short fat man, because he was helping his friend back to his feet.

"Get back here, kid. You're not getting away from us." The robust man pulled out a silver tube then blew into it, nothing happened so Zane continued to fly away. A loud popping noise off to one side sounded. Zane turned to look for the source of the noise and, upon instinct, Zane tried to fly away from the noise. Zane found himself instead being pulled by some unseen force to the side. The harder he pulled away, the faster he flew in that direction. The disruption was enough to send him crashing into a row of lockers screwed to the wall. Zane flew through the lockers and smashed into the concrete bricks instead. Before he could push himself away from the wall, Zane saw a balloon appear from below him, it popped, and he found himself being pulled down as well. Zane skidded along the floor but was able to pick himself up just as another balloon burst above and to his right. This time, instead of pushing away from the pull, Zane jumped towards it. This proved to be the right thing to do, as Zane felt little to no pull as he flew towards the spot. He let himself fall to the ground then took off flying once again. this time, he was able to escape the balloons as they appeared.

Risking a glance back, Zane was happy to see the little man out of breath, his face a beet red. His companion, however, looked ready for a fight. Zane watched as the man pulled out small shiny ball bearings. One shot from his hand and zoomed towards Zane who narrowly avoided the ball, as it embedded itself into the ceiling above him. A second later the ball exploded. Zane was knocked from the air. He rolled as he hit the floor, trying to avoid as much damage as possible. Ears ringing, Zane pulled himself up onto his feet. He watched as a second ball bearing flew from the man's hand. Zane braced himself for the inevitable impact. A large hand pushed Zane aside and grabbed the bearing out from the air. Zane watched as the dean hurled the ball back at the man. He jumped back looking surprised. The man scrambled away from the ball bearing; he didn't make it far, as the ball exploded, launching the man down the adjoining hallway.

"Glad to see you're awake. We need to keep moving. There is not a lot of time to explain what is going on," the dean said, while turning to run down the hall where he had presumably come from.

"Is that guy going to be okay?" Zane asked as they ran, feet pounding on the ground.

"Who? Blasty? He will be fine. He can't be blown up. Trust me, I've tried."

Zane nearly laughed knowing the man's name was Blasty, of all things.

"So, what is going on? How did you get back?" Zane asked.

"Zack was the one who got me back, but that is not important right now. Jane is planning something terrible; we have to stop her. Do you have your suit?" the dean asked.

"No, I don't have it, do you have yours?" Zane asked curiously.

"Yes, of course." As if to prove that he did, the dean pulled at his shirt. The flimsy material shredded off his body. Merely Justice appeared. He took off at a pace that Zane couldn't match, so Zane tripped himself and caught up.

"So, what's the plan?" Zane asked, getting excited.

"Try not to die and take down the enemy while doing the first part."

Zane now understood why Merely Justice was mainly just a sidekick.

"That's your plan?"

"Well, yeah, it's usually a good one. It's kept me alive this long."

"Well, at least tell me the rest; like what exactly is Jane planning?"

"I don't really know, but with Jane it isn't really safe to assume it will be something nice and pleasant."

"Did being trapped really do that much to your memory?" Zane asked.

"My memory is fine, it's just that I get too angry to listen when someone is threatening innocent children." He said while slamming a sledgehammer sized fist into the receiving hand. Zane swallowed hard, glad that he had never threatened any innocent children. They moved along the hallways for what seemed like an eternity. Until they met up with a vibrating and hovering Zack.

"Zane, brother, I wondered where you got off to," Zack said.

"What are you talking about? You deliberately left me to be picked up by the body incineration crew."

"Wow! They move fast," Zack said, looking surprised.

"So, what evil plan do we have to foil? Did Jane ever find Gliss? Did she come back and…" Zane trailed off as he realized that what he was about to ask was answered by the very people Jane had threatened to kill.

"Not sure if she ever found Gliss, but I don't think she had time. Once I'd freed uncle, he insisted that we leave you and find Jane to see what she is up to. He said something about you deserving it because you punched him or something," Zack said, shrugging his shoulders.

The dean smiled but Zane thought he noticed embarrassment at the added tidbit in Zack's story.

"So, we followed her to the council room, and she had a meeting with a group called..." The sound of a door being ripped out from the wall came from behind them. All three of them turned and watched as Gliss and their students stepped in. Zane tried to call out and wave a hand at her as she began down the hallway but to no avail. He looked at his once-covered hand then grimaced as he remembered the glove had been blown off in the fight with Blasty. Zane moved to follow the group, but a firm hand planted itself on his shoulder.

"They will be fine. The threat is ahead of us," the dean said, trying to reassure him.

Zane felt sick to his stomach as he watched them disappear down the dark hallway.

"Okay, continue, what do we have to do?" Zane asked, becoming impatient that this was the third time he had asked the same question.

"Right, of course. Well, we heard them talking about stealing something ancient from the school. They said it would change the balance of powers in the world. They called it the Omniousis Multiplier. It looks like a small silver cube that glows blue. I'm not sure what it does, but we do know where it is."

"The longer we wait, the better chance we have of losing that cube," the dean said.

"Where is it?" Zane asked.

"It is under the school, which was built upon ancient graves of people long ago and they left it there. That's all I can say."

The dean took off and Zack raced behind him. Zane hesitated then began to follow. They came to a large door set into the floor. The dean heaved a lever to one side and the stone beneath them began to shake as the door slid open. Zane held his breath waiting to see what awesome adventure awaited them. His excitement faded as the door revealed a dark hallway leading ominously down into an inky black void below.

Zane had read enough books and watched enough TV to know that this would end badly. The dean and Zack charged forward. Zane once again lingered, feeling the same emotion that pulled at him warning him that something was wrong. Zane knew that he needed to hurry, so he zoomed down the black hallway. The hallway stretched on for what seemed to be an eternity. Zane was forced to land as the hallways became claustrophobic to fly in. He also found the taste of spider webs distasteful. If he had to describe them, it would be like eating sugar-free cotton candy that didn't melt or have any flavor. Zane still hadn't caught up with Zack or the dean. He pushed himself to continue at the same pace he had before. His hard work paid off as he found the two holding the glowing cube. Two goons lay unconscious on the floor next to a pedestal. "Wait, it was that easy; no trap doors, no poison darts, no labyrinth of elaborate mazes?" Zane asked through ragged gasps.

"This isn't television, or a book. The ancient civilization who dwelt here were very simple people," the dean said smiling.

"Where is Jane?" They all looked at each other, then they heard the yelling.

"Zack, you gotta get me out of this dimension now, Gliss needs my help." Zane said frantically hoping his friend could do as he requested.

"Zane, I don't know if I can," Zack said, shrugging.

"Please."

"Fine, take my hands. Uncle, you may as well do the same now that we have recovered the cube."

Merley Justice begrudgingly agreed. Zack began to vibrate, Zane felt his teeth chattering, then the vibrations came so quickly, it felt like everything was going in slow motion. They stayed that way for a long time. Zane could hear different frequencies being reached, the sound increased, then the nausea hit. Zane nearly let go but pushed his body until there was a slight popping noise. Zack let go and fell backwards, sweat pouring from his head onto the ground. Zane looked around. The two goons were gone. Merely Justice waved a hand at Zane telling him to go quickly. Not caring whether or not he scraped his elbows, knees, or head. Zane took off flying as quickly as he could. He shot out of the tunnel, and into the hallways of the school. Zane headed down to where he'd last seen Gliss. He arrived just in time to watch as Jane fell through a mirror. Zane flew over to the mirror and tried to push his body through.

It didn't work, so he flew down the hallway remembering Ethan's power. He looked for any mirrors. Zane smiled as he looked into one next to a group of lockers. As he did, he saw Gliss in the reflection, so Zane followed checking mirrors until the school building ended. Zane slammed a fist into the wall. He turned around and found the nearest door. Zane smashed his face into the door as he tried unsuccessfully to fly through them. He rubbed his nose as he remembered that he was back in the real world. Zane tore the doors open, not caring about the alarm it set off. He took off in the same direction the group had been heading in. Zane flew and looked around. The other school buildings were in the opposite direction. There was no way of telling if Ethan's power would jump to the closest building or if it would be random. Zane froze hanging in the air, waiting and watching for commotion in the nearby group of buildings.

Zane heard a small crash and noticed the bank down the street. He raced towards the building but then noticed smoke rising from the building next door. Zane flew down to the front entry. As he was tugging on the door, it flew open, revealing some of his students. Henry was helping a coughing Ruby out of the building. Zane rushed forward and helped Henry pull Ruby out, away from the building. Zane watched in horror as the whole building shifted.

"Where is Gliss?" he asked Henry.

"She went after Jane, up above."

"Get the rest of the class as far away from the building as possible. Don't turn around for any reason, got it?" Zane yelled.

He was about to head into the building, when he noticed the rest of the students coming out of the door. He hoped Gliss would come out next. He frowned as she did not appear. Zane even watched as Simon and Logan carried some of the bad guys out of the building. Logan looked as if he were going to throw up. They didn't need to be told what to do as the building began to lean further.

Zane was about to rush into the building just as a boot landed next to him. Zane looked up. Gliss was the owner of that boot. He had designed it specifically for her. Zane took off upwards as the building began to crumble.

Zane whizzed through the air, dodging falling debris from the building next door. It was at times like this he wished his limits on flight were a little less strict. He changed direction in a flash, narrowly missing a large chunk of concrete roughly the size of a car. It fell and crashed into the asphalt below, leaving a gaping hole in the road. The sounds of metal straining trying to contain the now off-balance building, thrummed through the air around him. Zane continued to weave through the air, heading towards the top of the leaning building. Luckily it was after hours and there were no civilians in the building. The thought brought him little comfort as he made his way to the top. They failed. The building began to collapse. Zane willed his body to move faster through the air as he searched the rooftop looking for his friends. He spotted Gliss and Ethan clinging to the building. Gliss screamed as the building shook. Zane dove down towards his comrades and landed hard, as the building shifted toward him. Zane tumbled to the ground, knocking his elbows and knees on the concrete surface.

Shaking his head, Zane pulled himself to his feet and ran to his friends trying to overcome the daze of landing so hard. It was difficult to run on the slanted, rubble-covered rooftop. Zane's foot slipped on a patch of loose tile, and he hit the ground again, this time he began to slide towards the edge. Zane clawed at the surface and was able to come to a stop. Once again, Zane stood and made his way over to his friends. Gliss grabbed hold of Zane's arm, nearly throwing the two off the building. She cried and hugged him tightly, blood running down the side of her head from a gash. Her suit was torn on the arm sleeves, and she was missing a boot. Ethan called out towards them with hands outstretched and Zane noticed that the young man's eyes were completely swollen shut. *Drat!* Zane thought, *he can't use his powers. I'll have to carry them both.* Together Gliss and Zane made their way over to Ethan who was now clinging to a roof vent. Zane grabbed hold of the man as the building began to crash towards the ground. Gliss screamed and Ethan clung tightly to Zane as they lost their footing. Accelerating with all his strength, Zane leapt into the air. The added weight of his companions began to drag him down quicker than he'd expected. They plummeted towards the ground at an incredible speed, three screams sounding from depths of an all-consuming dust cloud.

Zane wanted nothing more than to hold onto Gliss, but her weight was just too much. Zane hoped the counter measures he had built into her suit worked, as he swung her around and launched her away from the building. He felt immediate guilt as he let her fingers slip from his. *Maybe she would think it was an accident,* he thought to himself. Zane tried not to breathe in as he pulled up with all his might. A boulder shot past his head nearly taking the two of them with it to the ground. Zane felt panic rise inside his chest as he knew that, even without Gliss, he wouldn't be able to pull up fast enough. Ethan was wearing a suit but, as Zane looked at it, he didn't think it was rated for more than a five-inch impact. Zane and Ethan hit the ground, Zane tumbled away and let his grip on Ethan slip. Zane felt like a rag doll as he flipped through the air, hitting what seemed like every rock on the ground, eventually his body came to rest.

Zane felt the pain. His brain didn't know where to tell him it hurt first because to be honest his whole body ached. Zane lay on the ground watching as the fine granules of dust fell on his face. The sun was nearly blocked by the plume that floated down through the air.

Suddenly, a green spark flashed through the dust connecting, every piece in an intricate design. The flash ended and the dust transformed. Zane watched as flower petals began to fall on his head. He smiled and quietly thanked RoseAnne. Zane didn't move for a long time. Despite his body protesting that it was not all right, Zane felt peace as he closed his eyes. A smile formed on his lips as he knew that they had saved their students. He changed his mind about having failed at their goal. It was silly to think they even had one. In the end, it had been their students who had risen to the task and had saved them. Zane kept the smile as he faded into the welcoming darkness that swallowed everything.

Chapter 21

New Beginnings

Zane woke up in what seemed to be the same hospital bed. He looked down and found Gliss snuggled into his chest. Zane had two casts; one on his big toe, and one on his left pinky, but he felt like the doctors could have placed his whole body in a cast as he rolled onto his side, as searing pain shot through his body and brought a stray tear to his eye. Zane noticed the shining metal handcuffs that linked him to Gliss who in turn was linked to the bed frame.

"Gliss… Are we?" Zane tried to ask, Gliss slowly rolled over.

"Did you say something?" she mumbled before her eyes widened and all grogginess vanished.

"Zane… how dare you! I'm never letting you fly me again; you dropped me… on purpose! You just be happy that the system worked, everything is fine except my right foot." Gliss lifted up her foot showing off her hot pink cast. Zane winced as he remembered the missing boot.

"I'm so sorry, I… I… I…" Zane stuttered. Gliss sat up, then kissed him, she pulled away.

"Thank you for saving my life," Gliss said. Zane remembered that she was not the only one on the roof top when they dove off.

"How is Ethan? Is he okay?" Zane asked.

"He fared better than me, not even a scratch," Gliss pouted. Zane felt the relief wash over him.

"And the rest of the class?"

"All fine, just some bumps and bruises."

"Are we under arrest?" Zane asked, gesturing to the cuffs.

"Oh yeah, totally. The dean showed up with the two goons, but the police arrested him too. The only one they haven't arrested is Zack, as they couldn't find him." Gliss said beaming.

Zane didn't know why being under arrest was a good thing. The day passed and soon Zane and Gliss were discharged from the hospital. The ride to the police station wasn't very glamorous, but at least they did get to ride together. They pulled up to the station and with a little help were escorted inside. Zane and Gliss were fingerprinted, then led over to the holding cell. He was surprised to find the dean and his father already inside the cell.

"Dad, what are you doing here?"

His father looked up.

"Oh, hello, son. It's great to see you, I'm not entirely sure… They did tell me something though. It's

271

hard to remember, I got hit in the head by a falling rock when I was walking into our bank to close out our old accounts."

The dean raised his eyebrow, and looked at Zane's father with new understanding.

"Wait, you're telling me you were there?" Zane asked.

"Hmm. At the bank? Yes, I didn't think it was unusual."

Gliss looked at Jerry in shock. Zane mouthed the words; I told you so.

"Where is Zack?" Zane asked the dean.

"With friends, can't be too careful. Somebody could be listening in."

Zane tried to prod for further information, but was met with the same answer. They spent the next week in the holding cell before all evidence was submitted and the prosecution made their decision. Zane was relieved when they only sentenced him and his class to building a new park for their community. Taking into account all the powers of his class, it was decided that a park should replace the building, and those who had actively participated in its demolition should split the responsibility. It took several days for his mother to convince the officers, her husband had nothing to do with the building's collapse or the mysterious disappearance of the students. All black clothing was taken and donated from his wardrobe to eliminate the slight chance he'd be mistaken for a bank robber again.

The dean lost his position at the school and was forced to wear a tracking anklet. The police removed the anklet once all the students and faculty were accounted for. Zack was made out to be a hero as the press found him rescuing the lost students and faculty. Zane understood what the dean meant when he said Zack was "staying with friends". He had been sent to retrieve the rest of the lost individuals from the sub dimension.

Zane was happy that his class had been there to help. He felt a warmth inside his chest as he walked up to join Gliss as they made their way into Jan's Café. She took his hand in hers as they opened the door together. Zane was happy to once more be greeted by the small problems in life, like not fitting through a door while holding hands. He smiled as they did an awkward dance to get in. Jan sprayed them with a flurry of praise, hugged them both and thanked them for all the new customers. Zane and Gliss were shown to their table.

"What took ya so long? You two can fly, right?" Henry asked. The others joined in and began to mercilessly tease Zane and Gliss.

"So, where do we go from here?" Ruby asked while shifting the table color to sea green.

"What do you mean?"

"I mean, what's next for us?"

Zane hadn't anticipated the question. He hadn't given much thought to what would happen next.

"I don't know, I guess we just go back to being normal," Zane said, shrugging his shoulders.

"Listen, we all have been talking it over. We have already filed the proper paperwork, and our application

273

has been accepted. We have our Hero's Licenses. And, since we all graduated early," Henry said using air quotes around the word 'graduated', "we want to be heroes. If these last couple months have taught us anything, it's that the world needs heroes. So, we have created the Lesser Heroes Hero Agency. Merely Justice has already agreed to be the CEO. We want you to work with us. What do you have to say?"

Zane sat for a long while without responding. He somehow felt guilty that they had to grow up so quickly. That he had been the one to risk their lives. The thought popped into his head, *if you don't join them, then it will be your fault.*

He looked at Gliss and she nodded her head. They raised their glasses full of blue cream soda and Zane toasted, "To the Lesser Heroes. May we bring peace to the world."

The rest of the meeting went by in a blur. Zane pulled on his helmet as they stepped outside. Gliss pulled hers on as well. It felt strange to not have to fly Gliss any more. She gave him a thumbs up, and together they twisted the communications knobs.

"Ready?"

"Ready."

They took off in an explosion of glitter. Zane hated getting left in the dust, but he simply lacked the power to keep up. His jet engine whined as he sped up trying to catch her. Soon they evened out and shot away, heading towards the mountains. The sunlight rested on the mountains, which set the sky ablaze. It was truly magnificent.

"Zane?"

"Yeah, Gliss?"

"Do you think Aunt Margery is all right?"

Zane felt taken aback, he had no good answer that could console her or soothe her worry.

"I don't know..." he said lamely. Then added, "but I can tell you this, the Lesser Hero Agency will find her and bring her back, no matter what!" trying to sound strong and confident.

"Thanks... I know we will."

With that they set their GPS coordinates, and flew towards the horizon into a rich and deepening sunset.

The End